OF GREED AND GLORY

E. A. OLIVIERI

Content Warning

Death, murder, descriptions of violence, gore and torture, descriptions of battle and killing, discrimination, alcohol use and addiction, on-page sex and sexual acts, depictions of mental health struggles and PTSD.

In the spirit of reconciliation I, E. A. Olivieri, acknowledge the Traditional Custodians of Country throughout Australia and their connections to land, sea and community. I pay my respects to their Elders past and present and extend that respect to all Aboriginal and Torres Strait Islander peoples today.
This book was written on Whadjuk Nyoongar Country.

OTHER TITLES BY E.A. OLIVIERI

Tales of Carynthia
Ashwood and Brimstone

For the readers that waited and continue to wait.

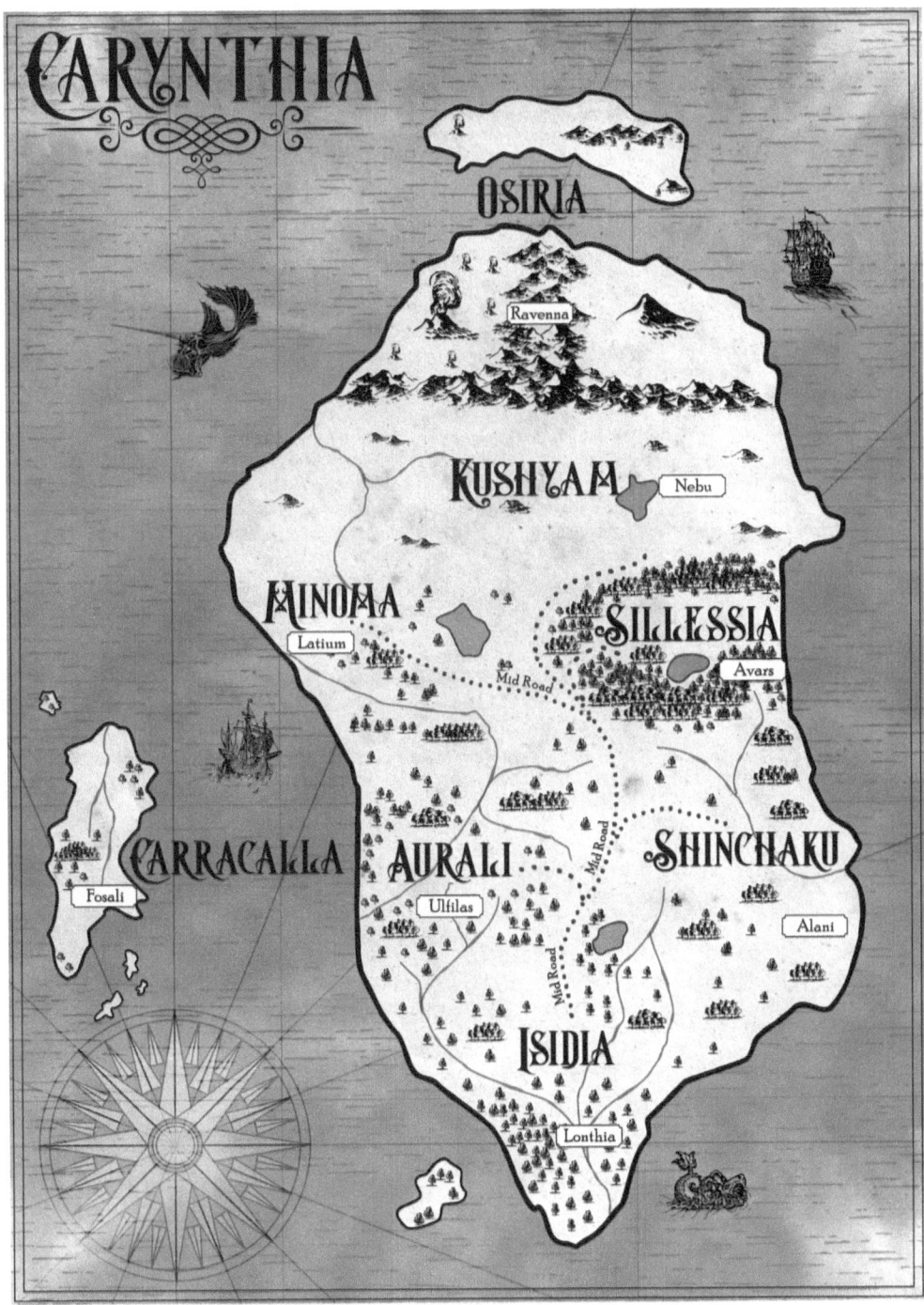

CARYNTHIA

OSIRIA

Ravenna

KUSHYAM

Nebu

MINOMA

Latium

SILLESSIA

Avars

Mid Road

CARRACALLA

Fosali

AURALI

Ulfilas

Mid Road

SHINCHAKU

Alani

Mid Road

ISIDIA

Lonthia

A BRIEF HISTORY OF CARYNTHIA

Before the humans and elves ruled Carynthia, there were only goblins and fairies. Created by the Mother and Father before all other beings, and gifted with Their magic, they lived in a kind of peace for a time, before the goblins grew angry with the fairies.

For fairies were creatures of chaos, much like their Mother, and did not respect the autonomy of others.

The Goblin Queen, sick of dealing with fairy meddlings, ordered an item to be made and enchanted to ward against fairy magic. Word of the enchanted object spread across Carynthia and into the ears of fairies.

Enraged by the resistance against their magic, the fairies declared war against the goblins.

The war raged for years, bloody and unforgiving, but the tide began to turn in favor of the goblins after they constructed an army of stone creatures enchanted to hunt and kill fairies. In an act of desperation, the fairies called upon a new race, a foreign race—elves.

They lived in a land across the sea, a sea filled with monsters that was too dangerous to cross without the assistance of fairy magic; but with it and the promise of great blessings, the elves crossed the sea and helped the fairies in their war.

The goblins' stone creatures stood no chance against the onslaught of the elves. Many lives were lost, the goblins dwindled in numbers and, in the harshest of ways, a new race was born—Orcs. Loathed by all, they served as a terrible reminder of the cruel happenings of war.

As payment for their services, the elves were given dominion over the land of Carynthia; four elves were chosen by the fairies to receive their blessing. The fiercest warrior, Osira, was gifted the power of death; her brother Isidan, a knowledgeable healer, was gifted the power of life. Sillesse, a proud farmer whose hard work had kept the armies fed, was gifted the power to imbue her crops with magic so that they would never fail; because of her caring nature, she was also gifted the ability to speak with all manner of land beasts. Last was Callan, the Master of Ships; he was gifted gills, allowing him to breathe underwater and the ability to speak to sea creatures so that he should never fear sailing the waters beyond.

The fairies' triumph was short-lived, however. For when the Father looked down on his wife's creation, he wept at the abuse of their powers and banished them to the dense woods. In retaliation, the Mother took the goblins' enchanting magic away but took pity on their dwindling numbers and left them free to reside in the mainland.

The four elves would go on to spread their magic through their lineage until we are left with the Carynthia we know now, ruled by humans and four new races of elves.

At last, after millennia of on and off war, the land of Carynthia had stumbled into the semblance of peace. The seemingly endless fighting between Isidia and Osiria had halted for the first time in centuries. The Queen of Isidia took this moment of quiet to marry the Prince of her longtime ally, Carracalla, solidifying the relationship between the two lands. Not long after, the union was blessed, and a baby was born.

The new King's family and all high ranking Isidians were invited to celebrate the blessing of the new Princess; a sacred occasion beseeching the gods to grant their favor to this child and aid in the establishment of a new dynasty that would change the very fate of Carynthia.

CHAPTER

I

I broke through the pile of cushions, sucking in a much-needed gulp of fresh air.

The sun was shining harshly through the open window, and I winced as the noise from the docks below echoed inside my pounding head. My stomach turned, and I feared I would lose its contents before I could make it to the window—or a chamber pot. I pulled myself up through the mountain of mismatched silk, tassels, and frills, being careful to climb over the pale, naked bodies and limbs of the Isidian paramours that had kept me company the night before. I might have still been legless, but that wasn't going to stop me appreciating the sight of bare breasts and buttocks in the morning. A body to my right rolled over and grabbed my ankle.

"Bellona, where are you going?" he asked. I couldn't remember his name, had we picked him up in the tavern or on the street?

"To piss and throw up, want to join me?"

He groaned and rolled back over. "Not into that."

I shrugged and continued on.

We'd started at the palace, a dinner with Eevan and Islina, then I left with some servants and headed into town, unable to stand the disapproving looks from my sister-in-law any longer. We'd drunk in the tavern for hours, smashing down tankard after tankard. I was then led to a back-alley den where we smoked some strange Aurali substance that left us senseless for only the Mother and Father knew how long, and then we'd ended here—the only whorehouse in the whole of Lonthia.

I sighed as I relieved myself over the chamber pot, my stomach settling a slight amount as the pressure on my bladder loosened. I stood for a moment, getting a feel for how my stomach was handling the abuse I'd inflicted on it the night before, trying to decide whether or not I should force myself to throw up to make myself feel better. I decided I was fine and turned around to assess

3

the damage to the room. There almost always was some kind of damage after a good night, especially when I was involved.

The Isidian brothel had multiple rooms, each one decorated to a different theme; the room we'd chosen last night was the Sillessian room. There was no bed, just hundreds of beautifully embroidered pillows, bright-colored curtains lined the walls and ceilings, mimicking the inside of a tent. What little furniture there was had been made in the same raw-style that real Sillessian furniture was. Like the chairs carved out of tree stumps that, from the back, still looked like a regular old stump; it was the same with the vanity toward the back of the room, where an Isidian elf was fixing her black hair in the dirty mirror. I frowned at the reflection in the mirror—I didn't remember her either. I usually made it a point to remember everyone I slept with, but the last night was a blur. All I could recall were flashes of limbs and the glorious sounds of pleasure.

The Isidian gave me a sour look through the mirror, as if I'd offended her somehow, but I was sure she hadn't thought that last night when I'd most likely had my face buried between her slim thighs.

My head rang as the bells from the temple sounded through the city, echoing painfully off stone buildings and walkways. A collective groan sounded from everyone in the room, followed by more heads bursting up through the mass of cushions, a few curses as some realized they were late for work or would be found missing by family or spouses. People began frantically dressing and leaving the room. I simply lit my pipe and lounged on the open window, watching the chaos unfold.

"For fuck's sake, Bellona."

I choked on my pipe smoke and reached for the nearest curtain to cover myself. "Darius! What the pit are you doing here?!"

"Looking for you in the only place you could be." My brother's eyes were fixed to the ceiling of the room. "You're late, hurry up and get dressed. Eevan is pissed."

"What for? I'm enriching his economy," I said, taking a drag from my pipe.

"And missing his daughter's blessing."

Fuck.

I pushed off the window sill and dug for clothes, any clothes that I could find that were half suitable for a blessing ceremony. If Eevan was pissed, Islina would be murderous, and I was already on her shit-list after leaving halfway through dinner last night. I threw on the first shirt I found, it was too tight on my arms and shoulders, the pants I found too big. Somehow, I managed to dig up my own boots in the mess. I dashed past Darius in the doorway, smoothing my hair back with the layer of grease that coated it from my hard night.

"You look like shit," Darius observed.

"Gee, thanks," I shot back.

We raced up the winding stone paths to the temple, the streets thronging with people longing to be included in the affairs of the royals, and pushed through the circle of guards keeping the people back, both of us breathless and covered in sweat.

I pushed the doors of the temple open and they slammed back against the thick marble pillars, the noise echoing through the sacred space. Every person in attendance spun to face me. Isidian courtiers, pale, black-haired and green-eyed, and my own people, Carracallans, gray-skinned, black-eyed, and blue-haired.

My shoulders sagged.

I offered a small smile to my brother and his wife, standing centered over the altar, their newborn nestled in their arms. I could tell Eevan was furious—then once he took in what I looked like, he looked as if he wanted to laugh. At me or the whole situation, I wasn't sure. Islina was seething, I was glad that we were in a sacred place. Otherwise, I truly believed she would have killed me.

Darius and I slipped up the side aisle, past rows of people seated on carved stone benches facing the white marble altar. The priest had resumed spouting his bullshit to the congregation, my brother listening intently to the ritual for his precious child.

"Bellona Glenon, you will make this up to your brother," my mother hissed as I sat beside her on one of the uncomfortable stone pews, pain shooting through my rear. Whatever alcohol or other substance that had remained in my system this morning had started to wear off, and I was beginning to feel the aftermath of last night. I shifted my hips so that I was sitting more on my left cheek.

"I know, I know." I waved her off. My head was pounding, sweat trickling down my brow.

"You smell horrendous, where did Darius find you? Actually, I don't want to know." She held up her hand, as if I'd planned on answering.

I rolled my eyes. I would never live this down.

"With this water, I bless this child under the watch of the Father, and with this fire, in the name of our Mother, the Mother of all and the Father of all. May they keep this child healthy and safe under their watchful gaze for as long as she may live."

My eyes began to flutter, my hands shaking. The priest's words began to muddle together in my head. I couldn't keep track of what part of the ceremony we were up to. It had been so long since I'd been to worship, it wasn't something we did in Carracalla, our connection to the sea meant more to us than the gods, who may have created it but had no control over it. I tried to chant with the other attendees, but found that I'd forgotten the words. I stood when I should have kneeled, and sat when I should have stood.

I struggled not to laugh at myself and Peverell, my other brother, sighing with frustration beside me every time I got something wrong. Islina's shoulders were rising higher and higher with each one of my mistakes, until they were practically touching her jaw.

No, this family event would not end well for me.

The ceremony ended with Eevan and Islina placing the baby's hands in a bowl each, one of cold water, which had shocked the babe into crying, and one warm, each symbolizing the Father and the Mother. The Priest said his last blessing over the baby, and the congregation rose to chant their response. I was late to rise, my head aching from the screams of my infant niece, and I'd forgotten the response.

So instead I mumbled some nonsense and crashed back down into my pew, sucking in a sharp breath as I sat flat on my arse and it kindly reminded me how much it hurt.

"I now present to you, Princess Evalina Elsrine Glenon of Isidia, blessed by the Mother and Father," The Isidian preacher proclaimed.

The crowd erupted with cheers.

I shrunk back from the noise, practically cowering behind my mother as my head throbbed.

Evalina, I almost laughed—it showed how lacking in creativity my brother and sister-in-law were. Elsrine, that I could let pass, a homage to her matrilineal lines. My mind got to thinking of what Queen Elsbeth could have been like, to have a daughter like Islina. She had either been absent or a brute, surely, to produce such a bitch of a daughter.

I followed my family as they exited the temple, not likely to enter another until the next niece or nephew was born. Instead of continuing with them to fawn over the baby and her newly revealed names, I walked to the side of the temple and emptied my stomach behind a bush. The rush of the morning had been too much after what I'd done to myself the night before.

"Bell."

I flinched, I was in for it now. "Eev, beautiful ceremony. Congrats on ... all that ... and what beautiful names." My charms had never worked on Eevan—we were too alike.

"You looked like you were going to shit yourself the whole time. Are you still drunk from last night?" He was trying to sound annoyed, concerned, but it came off more amused and ... maybe a little jealous.

"Not still drunk, and if I'd shat myself, I probably would have died," I joked, rubbing my sore arse.

Eevan pinched the bridge of his nose. "Bell, you're making this really hard for me. If you don't buck up, Islina's going to ban you from the kingdom."

"It was just a bit of fun! Come on Eev, you remember fun, right? We used to have it before your wife castrated you."

My brother's face darkened. "It's not funny, Bellona. This was the one day I wanted you present, for Evalina. I thank the Father that she, at least, will not remember this." He took a deep breath, his black eyes fixing on the blue sky above. "I want you to be part of her life, but Islina won't let that happen if you don't sort yourself out."

I rolled my eyes. "As if she could stop me." When his frown became more downturned and he made to reply, I quickly placed a hand on his shoulder. "I'm joking, brother! I'll be better. Last night was an accident, I didn't mean for it to go so far." I ruffled his blue hair. "I'll be better."

Eevan pulled away from me and tried to flatten his hair before returning to his wife and child. The brother I had once known was gone—he was a husband now, a father. We would have no more parties or adventures. My stomach churned as I watched him kiss his wife and steal his child away from her, gazing lovingly into his daughter's eyes.

They'd stolen him from me. My best friend. The only one that understood me.

I decided to walk up to the castle, ahead of the planned procession. Along with the now constant pain radiating from my arsehole, my legs were burning and my hips ached.

I must have had a great night. I wished I could remember it better.

The castle grounds of Lonthia were beautiful, I had to give Islina that—she knew how to look after a palace. The walls were clean, the white stones glowing so brightly in the sun it made my head throb to look at them. The garden was well maintained, nothing overgrown or creeping. In Carracalla, we cared more for our ships. The villages were mostly wooden shacks, the castle little more than a leaking ruin, but our fleets were a sight to behold. Even from the gardens of the palace, I could see them down in the docks, gleaming in the sun.

I could spot my baby, *The Siren's Shriek*, from any distance. She was my pride and joy, a gift from my brothers after completing my first voyage. It was an important coming of age tradition for my people; we had to complete a solo voyage to prove our strong knowledge of and connection to the sea. A tradition that made sense. We showed our respect to the sea—lest it swallow us whole—rather than spend time in a temple worshiping gods that couldn't give a rat's arse if we lived or died. There was not a scratch on her, not one single barnacle, and there never would be. My mother had cringed at the name when I'd excitedly yelled it the second the great ship was presented to me; it was a nod to her heritage, one she would never confirm but also never deny.

I hated to be on land, wasn't used to the stillness of it anymore, or how many people were … everywhere. I loved my crew, they were an extension of my family, but they stayed on the ship, doing maintenance and staying away from the properness of society. We were a rather improper bunch.

I let out a sigh under the judgmental gazes of the Lonthian servants on my back as I made my way to my rooms. I knew how it looked, that I was arriving before anyone else, but I'd rather get cleaned up for the rest of the event than be at my niece's blessing party smelling like alcohol, the unknown Aurali substance and sex.

I'd managed to bathe and dress before the rest of the party had made their way back to the palace. I felt slightly better after my bath, my head clear, my body relaxed after soaking in the hot water. My naval uniform was all I had that suited the formal occasion, with pale pants, hose, and waistcoat, and a deep-blue, double-breasted jacket that matched my hair perfectly. I'd slicked back my short locks with oil—it was too long to leave free—so I knew it and the gold buttons of my jacket gleamed in the afternoon light shining through the destroyed roof of the Isidian throne room that dimmed only when the shadow of the enchanted autumnal leaves, spelled to fall from the non-existent ceiling, swept over the party below.

I stuck to the edges of the room, smoking my pipe and waiting for my family to arrive, considering what to say to Islina to redeem myself—even slightly. I hadn't thought I'd done anything wrong at dinner, I was just trying to liven things up, and Islina had glared at me from the other side of the table the whole time. I'd thought she'd want to hear of Eevan's and my adventures, but clearly I'd kept one too many damning details in that should have remained withheld.

I didn't have a clear measure of what was deemed too improper by Isidian conventions, it was part of the reason that Eevan and I had grown so far apart after he'd begun courting Islina. I was too crass for her liking. People from the ceremony continued to trickle in, taking up space between the over-decorated tables, people I had no interest in conversing with. From the looks they threw me, I assumed they felt the same way. How lucky that I was fourth born, that no one was required to know me and I could be left to my own devices.

I tapped on the bowl of my pipe, sending embers flitting through the air before me. I reflexively blew them away from my face before they could float into my eyes, immediately realizing my mistake as they rose in the air, setting one of the leaves alight. I watched the leaf tumble through the air with my breath held, hoping it would land on the floor so I could stamp it out, but it swooped higher on a breeze from the open door.

My family entered the hall, Islina trailing behind Eevan, baby Evalina raised above his head, as the table closest to me was suddenly ablaze. I snuffed my pipe with my thumb and threw it to the ground as I rushed to pat out the flames. Shouting servants rushed over, calling for buckets of water, then splashing them over the table to put out the fire and saturating me in the process. I spun to apologize to my family, my brother, but Islina was already there, her face contorted with rage.

"Get out," she hissed.

"It was an accident, I'm sorr—"

"Get. Out." She ground out, hands shaking at her sides.

My face fell. I looked to Eevan, his face stern. I dropped my hands and walked around my sister-in-law towards the door. My shoulders caved inward as I felt the eyes of the other guests follow me to the entrance. Darius and Mira, her hands resting on her large pregnant belly, gave me sympathetic looks that said, 'we'd join you if it didn't mean Islina would come after us next'. I shrugged at them and continued to the doors.

"Bellona? Where are you going?"

I cringed at my father's voice. He was leaning against a pillar at the entrance of the hall, smoking his own pipe. "Islina kicked me out," I said bluntly.

He took a drag and held the smoke in his mouth for a long while before releasing it. "Did you really want to be here anyway?" He asked as if he already knew the answer.

"Well, I wanted to be here for Eev, and he wanted me here for Evalina."

He puffed on his pipe again. "Your brother knows you well enough to know you mean no harm. Islina will learn, too, just give her time." He gave me a one-armed hug, forcing the air from my lungs. "We're family, after all, the only family she's got," he added solemnly. "Go to the tavern, or wherever it is that you go, celebrate your way." He winked at me before snuffing his own pipe as

I had and entering the hall, Eevan's calming voice echoed out—he was giving a speech. No doubt thanking everyone for attending and apologizing for his disruptive, destructive little sister. At least my father understood. He knew I didn't do these things out of spite or need for attention. They just happened, as if I had been born destined for a life of chaos.

CHAPTER
2

The sun was setting by the time I'd collected coin from my room and begun my descent back into the village and I was glad for it. A cool wind blew up from the docks, halting any sweat forming on my brow.

I kicked a stone as I walked, imagining it was Islina's head, wishing it was that simple to free myself from her. She'd hung around our family like a bad smell for years. First pining after Darius until he'd met Mira, then constantly asking for assistance from my father after her parents died in the war—I guess that I could understand—and then she'd realized Eevan, who had been pining after her for what felt like centuries, wasn't too lowly of a person for *Her Majesty* to consider. And so she'd stolen him from me.

We'd done everything together before her, had been the best of friends. I should've been happy for him, but something deep in my gut burned every time I saw them together.

I took a seat at the bar of the first tavern I came across and ordered three drinks for myself, skolling the first two and sipping on the third, contemplating my brother's words. I did want to be there for my niece, Father knows she'd need someone fun in her life, but was it worth dealing with Islina? My father's words echoed through my head, 'the only family she's got'. I picked at the rough wood of the bar top and sighed. He was right, I should make more of an effort with her, especially if I wanted to see my niece and my brother.

I winked at the barman as he filled my tankard, receiving a blush and quick grin before he turned to service his other patrons. Was my body ready for more sex? After a quick assessment, I settled on yes, as long as we stayed away from my arse. I'd need a few days to recover that.

"Hard day?"

I scoffed at the male next to me. "I'm surprised the gossip hasn't reached you all down here yet."

"Oh, it has. I was being polite." He chuckled into his tankard. "Did you really try to set the palace on fire?"

I rolled my eyes at the exaggeration. "It was an accident. That whole throne room is a fire hazard."

The Isidian laughed again and signaled to the barman to refill his drink.

"You like to knock it back, don't you?" he asked.

"S'pose so," I replied, having a mouthful of my own drink.

"Then why don't we make this a little more interesting? Put a smile back on that glum face of yours."

My brows rose. "And what do you have in mind?"

He signaled for the barman. "How about a drinking game? From what I hear, you're not one to run from a little competition. Whoever can drink the most wins," he said with a snide grin.

I laughed. "What could you possibly have to offer me?"

"See, it's already working! Everything in my coin purse, and"—he dug around in his coat, too thick for the current weather, and slammed a roll of parchment on the bar—"a map to ancient goblin treasure, from a time before elves had arrived here."

My brows rose as I moved to retrieve the map for inspection, but the Isidian snatched it away with a pale hand.

"I'm to believe you without seeing it for myself?"

"A little mystery only adds to the fun and, really, what have you got to lose?" He shrugged.

My fingers tapped the side of my tankard as I considered. "And what's in it for you?"

"How about"—he tapped a pale finger on his chin—"the contents of your coin purse and your company for the rest of the night." A boozy smirk slid across his face.

"Barkeep," I called, "how many's he had?"

The barman thought for a second. "Same as you, once you finish that." He nodded at my ale.

I slammed it down, belching loudly as it sunk into my stomach.

The Isidian and I moved to a different table so that we were sitting across from each other and had the bar staff set it with rounds of spirits. We'd both already drunk four tankards of ale and decided twenty shots would be a good amount but would only stop drinking after one of us either threw up or passed out.

I took the first shot, staring into the green eyes of my competition, ignoring the others around us now placing bets.

When we each had five shots left, we were both swaying in our seats. We'd had multiple bathroom breaks, with someone following us in to make sure we weren't forcing ourselves to throw up—there's nothing quite like having someone watch you piss.

Damon, my competitor, had begun getting more and more irate the more he drank, picking fights with people he heard placing bets against him.

"You know who that is, right?" One laughed. "I'm not betting against Bellona Glenon in a drinking game." My supporters in the crowd cheered.

I straightened in my chair, reaching for my sixteenth shot of spirits. I held in the urge to laugh as the room around me seemed to ripple, distorting the faces of those surrounding me. I knocked back the shot and everyone went silent, watching and waiting to see if it would be the one to take me down, but I was fine. Damon gave an irritated grunt as I placed my shot glass back on the wooden table.

"Fuck." He sighed as he leaned forward to reach for his next shot and knocked one over in the process, the liquid spilling over his lap. Damon hissed as his hand continued to sway before him. I stopped myself from grinning at my impending win.

He finally managed to pick up a glass but sloshed the liquid down the sides and fell forward onto the table, splashing me with the contents of his drink. I pushed away from the table and brushed the liquid off my pants.

"I suppose that means I win!" I announced to the crowd and was met with an equal number of cheers and groans as people collected and lost their bets. I swooped around the table, and with a small knife that had been hidden in the lining of my coat, cut Damon's coin purse from his belt and fished the map from his jacket. I gave the money to the barman and left. I'd had my win for the night, and Damon had been right, the little competition had lightened my mood. But it was time to turn in before things got out of hand … again.

I had planned to go straight to my rooms, but my drunken mind told me to seek out Eevan—even though he was pissed with me. I shushed a set of decorative armor that collapsed to the ground as I stumbled down a palace hallway, shaking off the hands of servants trying to assist me. A loud bang rumbled through the library as I opened the door and fell through it. The carpets were soft beneath my bare feet as I fumbled my way through the vast room, leaning on bookshelves to keep myself upright and leaving a trail of books in my wake. Where had my boots gone? Why was everything so white? I pitied the servants that had to keep Lonthia clean.

"Shit!" I exclaimed as I fell into a large candelabra and it clattered loudly to the ground, the candles tumbling out and scattering across the floor. I raced after them on my hands and knees, patting out the flames that survived the fall.

"Bellona, what are you doing?" Peverell hissed, coming around the corner of a bookshelf, his arms loaded with tomes.

"Looking for our brother, brother," I said, collapsing into a fit of laughter. Someone down another aisle shushed me, clicking their tongue indignantly when I shushed them back.

"Bell, we're in a library," Peverell said, placing his books down and hauling me to my feet. "Keep it down a little."

"What is going on over here?"

Peverell and I cringed at the angry tone of our brother's voice—it was not something we were used to from Eevan, our fun brother.

"Eev! Look, look what I won!" I pulled the map from my coat and pressed it into his chest, using him to keep myself upright. He took hold of my arm and passed the map to Peverell.

"Bellona, I thought we talked about this. Father said he'd had words with you—does nothing stick?"

"It was one drinking contest. My last," I added at his disappointed look.

"Bellona, this is only part of a map," Peverell said from behind me, studying the map under the light of a candle.

"What?!" I pushed off Eevan and snatched the map from Peverell. "That fucker!"

"Alright, Pev, let's get her out of here before the mages kill us."

Peverell and Eevan took either arm and half lifted me to drag me from the library as I loudly ranted about being duped by the prick at the tavern.

Eevan's office here was a homage to our home. The walls were lined with paintings of ships at sea and the cliffs of Carracalla, the bookshelves held volumes on sailing and charting, and the sextant my parents had gifted him after his first voyage sat proudly in the center of the shelf. His desk was littered with papers and broken quills and in the corner, behind his large, kingly chair, sat the helm of his first ship, which he'd crashed into a cliffside after only having it for a month. I slumped into a chair that sat opposite his, Peverell taking the one to my left, continuing to study the map.

"So, you didn't think to check the map before entering into a competition?" Eevan scolded.

"The prick wouldn't let me see it, but does it matter? I would have been drinking anyway."

Eevan sighed. "Bell, you're making this really hard for me. Islina almost threw *me* out of the castle after you nearly burned it down."

"I didn't nearly burn down the castle. I put it out before it spread."

"That reminds me, you left this." Eevan pulled my pipe out of his pocket and passed it to me.

I took it from him and began packing the bowl with tobacco, more out of habit than need. "Thanks."

"Try not to set my office on fire."

"Oh, *fuck off*, Eevan," I said, lighting my tobacco with a candle and dripping wax on his desk in the process. "I'm sorry, alright? I'm sorry I've come here and disrupted your perfect life, with your perfect wife and child in your perfect kingdom."

Eevan paled. "Bell, that's not what I meant—"

"Well, that's how it comes across. You're a married man now, a king to someone else's kingdom, and a father—you don't have time for your shitty mess of a little sister. I get it."

"Bellona, that's not it at all."

"This is a goblin map," Peverell announced.

Eevan and I ignored him.

"You need to take better care of yourself and set a better example. You have a niece now and soon another, or a nephew. I would rather like it if you were around to see them grow up, not dead in a whorehouse somewhere. You can't expect us to keep looking out for you forever."

The words sobered me. Is that really what my family expected?

"Hey guys, this map is really fascinating."

"Pev, we're kind of having a serious discussion here."

"Bellona, I think you've actually found something worthwhile," Peverell said, pulling a notebook from his pocket.

"Really?!" I pushed him aside and gazed at the map, completely dropping the conversation I'd been having with Eevan.

I couldn't read any of the text on the map—it was written in ancient goblin symbols that I'd never learned. They could be found all around Carynthia, carved into old trees and rocks. The map depicted the lower half of Carynthia: Isidia, Aurali, Carracalla, and Shinchaku. I should have realized it was too small to be a full map, but the lure of alcohol and escapism had been enough to distract me from that fact. There was a large passage of writing in the lower corner of the parchment and a small symbol on a place in Shinchaku.

"What does it say?" I asked, pushing the map back into Peverell's face.

"Give me a second," he muttered, his charcoal scratching quickly across the page of his notebook as he deciphered the text. "If I've translated this correctly, it says something about a goblin treasure that was deemed too powerful by the first elves and hidden away. I can't translate it all right now, but I think this marker shows where the rest of the map is." Peverell pointed to the small symbol.

"There's no indication of what the treasure could be?" Eevan asked, shrugging at my incredulous glare.

"This is very vague but, if I'm remembering my goblin runes correctly, I believe it could be a bracelet made for the Goblin Queen during the first war. It was a ward against fairy magic—very powerful," Peverell said, leaning back in his seat. "It would be a priceless treasure, could teach us so much about the fairies."

"Or how to harness their magic," Eevan added.

My gaze danced between my two brothers, their expressions matched in thought. One no doubt considering the adventure and benefits of the treasure, and the other the unknown secrets that could be discovered. Harnessing fairy magic could mean so much for a kingdom, it would almost guarantee their success in any battle— if it could be truly controlled. Fairies were chaos beings, aligned fully with the Mother, which was why the Father had banished them to the Sillessian forests— to limit the reach of their magic and make Carynthia safe for the other races. But, in return, the Mother had stripped the goblins of their magic; now, tens of thousands of years later, very few goblin enchanted items remained.

"So … when do we leave? We're going after it, right?" I asked Eevan excitedly, barely keeping my rear in my seat.

"Leave for where?"

"For Shinchaku! We need the other half of the map."

"We don't even know if this map is real," Eevan said, running a hand over his face.

"Oh, it's definitely real," Peverell muttered, scanning the map.

Eevan looked between Peverell and I, at his desk laden with papers and court documents. "I … I-I can't leave," he finally said, defeated. "I would love to, Gods know I would love to, but I can't."

"Eevan, come on! I can't do this without you. One last adventure, for old times' sake," I said, rising from my chair and holding my arm out to him. "Think of what this could mean for Isidia."

"I can't … Islina needs me, Evie needs me."

I retracted my arm. Deep down, I knew he was right, but I couldn't help but feel, once again, as if they'd stolen him from me. "Then I'll go alone. My first solo voyage since I earned *The Siren's Shriek*."

Eevan's eyes lit up. "Why don't you take Pev?"

Peverell snapped out of his daydreaming. "Huh?"

"Go with Bell on her voyage! It'd be great! She runs the ship, you translate the maps"—he clapped his hands together, making us both jump—"you both find the treasure."

"Why am I being dragged into this?"

"Yeah, why are you dragging him into this?" I asked incredulously. Peverell and I had never been close. He was too quiet and scholarly, and I too … me.

"It's a great chance for you to get out of the books and see the world, Pev! And, who knows? Maybe he can sort you out a bit," Eevan said, throwing me a wicked grin. "Set you on the right course."

He knew exactly how this would go. I would be doing all the work and Peverell would be below deck stressing about his precious pages getting wet.

Peverell and I shared a look.

"I don't know about this, Eev," Peverell said, foot tapping on the stone ground.

"Just stay out of each other's way and you'll be fine. You need Peverell to read the goblin texts, or you won't find anything," Eevan pointed out, crossing his arms and sitting back in his obnoxious chair.

He was right and he knew it. Even if he could come with me, we'd still have to bring Peverell with us to translate. At least then there'd be a buffer, Pev and I alone together would probably not go as smoothly as he was expecting.

"Come on, Bell, for me. Do it to prove to me that you'll make an effort," Eevan said.

"You don't trust me to do it by myself?" I challenged.

"To be completely honest, no. I really don't. Peverell would be the perfect influence on you, and you him."

"Me? Why do I need influence?" Peverell asked, clearly offended.

"You're boring, Pev. You need to have some fun! Bellona can help you have fun and you can keep her under a certain amount of control." Eevan held his arms out like a priest accepting prayer from the congregation. "Do it for me, document it so I can read it and live through you."

Peverell thought on this for a moment, his foot tapping more aggressively. He glanced between the map, Eevan, his notebook, and me. His eyes settled on me, my wet clothes, messy hair, tobacco-stained fingers and alcohol breath. He sighed. "Fine, I'll do it."

Eevan grinned and turned his attention to me, waiting for me to say the same words, to agree to his plan.

"I'll do it, then," I said reluctantly. "But, on my ship, I am the Captain. I don't care how much older than me you are, you listen to my orders and you follow them." I jabbed a finger at Peverell to emphasize my point, not that I needed to make it. Carracallans knew to follow the Captain's orders, always.

Peverell nodded and held out his hand to me. I gazed at it for a moment, a small amount of regret lingering in my mind before I spat on my hand and smooshed it into his. He pulled his away with a cry of disgust that left Eevan and I as laughing heaps on the cold floor

CHAPTER

3

I knocked on my brother's door before bursting through it as the sun was rising the next morning.

"Come, Peverell! It's time to go," I said, pulling the curtains apart and letting in the early morning sun.

"Ugh, Bellona," Peverell groaned. "How are *you* awake?" he questioned, throwing his blanket over his face.

"Adventure never sleeps. Now—come, come, brother! It's a long walk to the docks." I threw his clothes at him and walked back to the doors. "I'll meet you in the entryway in twenty minutes."

Peverell groaned again and, as extra motivation to get him out of bed, I strolled down the hallway without closing his doors.

I hadn't needed to wake him up, or leave so early in the morning, but after the mess of the day before I longed to be back on my ship—with my crew, with people who understood me and accepted me for who I am. I walked through the palace to the royal quarters, hoping to find Eevan, but there was only Islina and the baby. I stood awkwardly in the doorway, unsure whether or not I wanted to test Islina after the events of the Blessing.

"Are you coming in or not?" Islina demanded from within.

"I-uh ... I guess so," I replied sheepishly, stepping through the doorway.

The rooms were filled with morning light. The windows on the eastern wall sat open, letting in the light morning breeze. Islina sat with the baby on the rug before the unused fireplace. She hadn't dressed for the day yet and wore only her nightgown, her black hair still disheveled from sleep—if she had slept. The deep circles under her green eyes told me she probably hadn't. In this moment, she looked most beautiful to me, more beautiful than when her hair was brushed and done up, her pale skin powdered to be perfectly paper-white and her form contorted smaller with a corset. She looked more attractive unrestricted in only her nightgown with her hair down, sitting casually on the rug as she was. I'd never really seen what my brother had found attractive in her, her attitude always blinding me, but now I saw her true beauty.

"You're leaving, then?" she asked shortly.

"Did Eevan tell you?" I asked, sitting across from her on the floor.

She nodded. "Told me of the great treasure, too. How his eyes lit when he spoke of it," she mused. "He would love to join you."

"He would rather be here with you two."

Islina gave a small, sad smile. "I would like to believe that. But Eevan's one true love will always be the sea."

Her words stumped me; Islina had never been so candid with me. I looked down at the babe, her thin arms reaching up for her mother's wiggling finger. In the morning sun, the small amount of hair on her head shone blue.

"I think he has some of the sea here with him," I said stroking the babe's head. *Evalina.*

Islina smiled. "I hope it stays like that—a small piece of home for him to have here." She paused for a moment, an emotion I couldn't read crossing her face, before she asked, "Are you sober?"

"Uh ... mostly." She raised an eyebrow and I shrugged. "I haven't had anything to drink this morning."

She seemed to take that answer enough and scooped up the baby, little Evalina, and placed her in my arms, adjusting my hold so that I was supporting her head and bottom. I gaped at Islina, at the baby, and back again.

"I know it seems like I hate you, and I'm not just saying this because Eevan absolutely tore me apart last night about how I'd reacted yesterday," she added with a sheepish grin, "but I don't. I envy you, so much, more than you could imagine." She took a deep, shaking breath. "It's hard for me to admit. But you seemed to have everything I didn't—endless fun and lack of responsibilities, people falling at your feet, a loving family, and Eevan." She paused again, gazing at her babe in my arms.

"He adores you, he's constantly gushing about his *'amazing little sister'* and telling stories of your adventures, adventures he'd never dream of taking me on." She reached forward and ran a finger down Evalina's cheek. "When Evie was born, one of the first things he said was 'I can't wait for Bell to meet her', he was so excited. I just wished for a moment that it could be *us*, just the two of us in that moment, that precious first moment ... but he still wanted you." Her eyes flicked to mine, reading my face for my reaction, but it was blank, I didn't know how to react. "I suppose it's because I don't have siblings, I could never understand the relationship between brother and sister, could never understand how two people can be so close and so alike. I've never had that—even with Eevan. We're opposites, and sometimes I feel as if I've suffocated him, trapped him in a life he didn't want, a life that's too boring for him." She stopped again, looking at me as if waiting for me to confirm her fears.

"Islina, if there's one thing I know about my brother, it's that he wouldn't do anything if he didn't want to. He loves you, and he definitely loves her." I smiled down at Evalina's plump little face, so much bigger than her tiny body.

"I would bet my life that he loves the two of you more than he could ever love the sea, or anything else for that matter. And, I suppose, I have to admit that I've been jealous of you, both of you," I added, smooshing my nose into Evalina's belly and was rewarded with a small smile. "I felt as if he'd abandoned me for you, as if maybe I'd become too much for him. I'm sorry for how I acted yesterday. I made a fool of myself and of you, and I'm going to do better. I don't want you to have to ask if I'm sober before you hand me my niece, and I don't want you to keep her from me."

Islina rested a hand on my shoulder. "You're not alone in this. We're here to help you but, and I feel I have to be blunt about this, if you ever come here in the state you were in yesterday again you will not be welcome back. Your father may go easy on you, and your brothers and mother may ignore it, but I will not. You're killing yourself, Bellona, with each sip and draw, and it's infuriating to watch. Losing you would destroy Eevan—I will not allow it."

I placed Evalina gently on the floor, just as she had been before, and pulled Islina into a tight hug. There was a moment of confusion before her arms eventually came around me, too. She said it would destroy Eevan, that my actions affected only him, but I understood her true meaning. "I'll be better," I said into her ear, "I promise. And Peverell is coming with me, anyway," I said as I pulled away. "I'm not going to get up to much with him around."

Islina laughed. "If there's anyone that can kill a mood faster than me, it's Peverell."

A barking laugh shot out of me. I'd never heard Islina make a joke, let alone a self-aware joke insulting one of my brothers. "We'll see how well he does when I return," I said, rising to my feet and poking one of Evalina's plump cheeks as I went.

"Good luck, Bellona," Islina said as I closed the door to her chambers.

"'*Meet me at the entry in 20 minutes*'," Peverell said in a mocking tone as I approached him.

I gave him a light punch on the arm. "I was saying goodbye to our niece."

"Islina let you near her? I'm surprised." I reached over and flicked his ear. "Ouch—piss off, would you?"

"Enjoy it while you can, brother, soon you won't be able to speak to me like that."

Peverell rolled his eyes and pulled his large pack onto his shoulders, the books inside thumping against his back.

"Gods, how many books have you got in there, Pev?"

"Many, and not all of them mine, so if we could hurry."

"Peverell, are you stealing books from our dear sister-in-law?"

"Only goblin related ones. Now let's go before the mages catch me."

I laughed as we made our way down the hill and to the docks, my ship awaiting us.

Peverell hadn't complained as we'd walked, but his gray face was tinged red and coated in sweat as we boarded *The Siren's Shriek*. The crew was already bustling about the ship, readying for cast off. I was confused until I spotted Eevan standing at the helm, toying with the wheel and staring out at the horizon.

"Taking orders from others now, are we?" I said, stepping on board from the gangway.

"Well, he is the King, Captain," my first mate said.

"Not your king, Jarrell. Take my brother and his stolen books to the stateroom," I directed, striding past him and taking the stairs two at a time up to the quarterdeck. "Eevan, what the pit, man? Taking over my ship?"

Eevan snapped his attention away from the horizon and onto me. "Sorry, Bell. I was just excited, I guess."

"Mm, don't make a habit of it."

"Got everything you need?"

"Should do. How about you?" I asked.

Eevan sighed, his hand tightening on the wheel. "Yes, I do." He smiled at me. "Got everything I need right here," he said with a sweeping gesture to the Isidian town before us, Lonthia Palace resting in the trees high on a hill above. "Did you see your niece before you left?"

"I did, and spoke to your wife."

His face paled. "And how did that go?"

"Fine, we've talked it all through and she's tentatively forgiven me—I think," I said, realizing she never outright forgave me.

Eevan laughed. "That sounds like her, you won't know if she truly has unless nothing happens—or it's too late. But I'm glad you spoke. I'm glad you saw Evie."

"I'll see her again, once I return with the treasure," I said, smacking his shoulder roughly.

"I hope she turns out like you." He paused and thought for a bit. "To a degree. I want her to have the best life, better than her mother's."

"Will you have more?"

"Not till Evie is older. The Council is already pushing for us to have a son, an heir—so old-fashioned. But I think Evie will be a great Queen. 'Queen Evalina Elsrine Glenon' sounds good, doesn't it?" he said, eyes sparkling in the morning sun.

"That's a lot of pressure to put on a baby," I said, half-joking. It was obviously expected of royalty, I'd just been lucky enough to be born last.

"I have a feeling about her, she's meant for something more than just a princess to be married off."

"I'm glad Isidia has you around, maybe you'll help this place advance like the rest of us have."

Eevan laughed. "Maybe." He ran a hand through his blue hair, gazing once again over the horizon. "Well, I better let you leave. There's treasure to be found. Travel well, Bellona," he said, gripping my forearm and pulling me into a tight hug, "and look after our brother."

"I will. We'll return here once we've got the bracelet." It didn't need to be said, but it comforted my own mind to have it known that the prize would be as much his as mine, as all things were (now) between Carracalla and Isidia.

With that, Eevan left me on the quarterdeck to say his farewells to Peverell and then left the ship; he took a place on the docks, resting against a crate, to wait and watch us sail away.

"Jarrell! How are we looking?" I called over the deck.

"Well, Captain, crew is accounted for, but we've got a new cook."

"What happened to our cook?" He'd only been with us for five years.

Jarrell shrugged. "New fellow is Halen, Isidian."

"Right. Riston! Ready to go?"

"Aye, Captain! Provisions were restocked yesterday, riggers were sent by the King this morning. I've just checked over their work and all seems well."

"Seems well or *is* well, sir?"

"*Is* well, Captain," he corrected. "Everything is ready to go."

"You know our heading?"

My Bosun nodded.

I clapped my hands, "Then let's go."

Riston blew his whistle, demanding the crew's attention. "All hands, prepare to disembark! Starboard fore braces! Port main and mizzen braces!"

The crew dissolved into groups, ten stood at the anchor chain waiting for the order to weigh, as others flocked to the starboard and port braces. I stood on the quarterdeck, admiring the organized chaos. Cast off was always my favorite part of the journey—spirits were high, excitement in the air. I lit my pipe, resting back against the starboard bulwark, admiring the morning bustle of the town, waving at the children that crowded on the docks to watch the ship leave. Closing my eyes, I sucked in a deep breath of salty air, the brine tinged with the light scent of petrichor hinting at incoming rain, before taking a long drag on my pipe.

"Weigh anchor!" Riston called.

Further grunting filled the air as the ten crew worked the wheel and hoisted the anchor. The wind picked up, filling the sails as if the Father himself was blessing our voyage.

I stood on the deck, staring back at the town as we sailed east to Shinchaku, watching it shrink into the distance, my brother's blue hair shining in the summer sun.

CHAPTER
4

Wind and rain lashed my face harder than any disgruntled lover's slap ever had. I stood at the helm, fighting with the wheel as the fierce currents pulled at the rudder beneath the surface of the water.

"Captain! Shouldn't we call it for the night?" Jarrell called over the blustering winds.

"No! The wind is perfect and I don't want to be blown off course!" I called back, shaking my hair off my face as a wave smashed over the bulwark of the quarterdeck.

"Captain, I'm sorry to say, but the crew can't handle it like you can. They're drowning out there!"

I gazed over the deck, as far as my eyes could see through the unforgiving deluge, my crew was clinging onto any part of the ship they could for dear life, their lifelines barely offering any sense of security, half of them gasping for air and the others choking on seawater. "Fine! Get below deck, you ninnies! I'll keep us going alone."

"I don't agree with that, Captain," Riston said, gripping the other side of the wheel. "I'll stay with you."

"I'll survive if I go overboard, *you* won't, get below deck."

"Are you saying you wouldn't save me?"

"Just get below deck! I can handle it."

He looked for a moment as if he was going to challenge me, but thought better of it. He knew as well as I did he'd drown where he stood in minutes if he stayed, the rain and spray from the sea leaving no gap to suck air. But I didn't need my lungs, didn't need to suck in air from my nose and mouth. I unbuttoned my jacket and threw it aside, baring the gills on my neck for the first time in weeks. I sighed as the rain hit them fully, moistening the surface. It was a blessing, a gift from the Father that I had been born with them, the first Carracallan in millennia to have gills. I took it as a sign of my worthiness, and perhaps that's where my problems began.

I'd always felt worthy, I'd never had to work for it as others did. Even my first voyage had been an easy one, I was not filled with the nerves and fear that others are because, even if I did fail or capsize, I would survive. There was no limit to how long I could be above or below water, I was only at the mercy of the creatures of the sea and, even then, most appreciated my wit or were too surprised to feast on me. But now, the life of my crew and my brother was in my hands. I could have, probably should have, reefed the sails, lowered an anchor and let the storm carry us slowly and safely through the night. But my mind was restless, my fingers itching for something to do, anything to distract me from the barrels of drink rolling in the hold.

I was lurched portside by a sudden gust of wind, almost loosening my hold on the handles. I pulled the wheel back up, my arms straining against the pull of the rudder. I had to keep us on course. The storm, too, was a blessing from the Father, I was sure of it. It was the only sense I could come to that the winds were traveling in the exact direction that we needed. He knew I was strong enough to stay on deck during it, that I alone could steer us through. I tightened my grip on the wheel and leaned my body into it more, holding it steady despite the current so desperately trying to spin it out from under me. I would be exhausted in the morning; I just had to hope that the storm passed by then.

My crew began emerging in dribs and drabs as the sun rose over the eastern horizon. The storm had passed overnight and, while I could have gone to rest when it did, I'd been too energized from winning my battle with the tides. I'd stayed up all night charting the stars as the clouds had cleared to be sure we were still on the right path, that my efforts hadn't been for naught.

"Bell, Were you up here all night?" Peverell said, walking up the steps to the quarterdeck.

"Ye—"

"During the storm?! Do you have a death wish?" he demanded.

"I think you mean *Captain*, Peverell, and on my ship I do what I want," I said, rising to my full height. "If you want to stay on this ship, brother, I would recommend not disrespecting me in front of my crew." I nudged my head, directing him to turn around.

He did, and paused when he beheld my crew all staring at him, waiting for my order to drag him below deck. "You are not their prince on my ship—barely even my brother—you're just a passenger, and passengers that disrespect their Captain get thrown in the brig."

He turned back to face me, his brotherly authority screaming at him to lash out.

"You've been away from the sea for too long, you forget your place."

The blow struck; Peverell's face fell. It was the worst insult you could give a Carracallan, to imply they've lost their connection to the sea. He turned away from me and stalked back to his rooms, the angry eyes of my crew following him as he crossed the deck.

"Back to work!" I called, and multiple bodies jerked into motion over the deck—the entertainment of the morning was over.

"How are we looking, Captain?" Jarrel asked.

"Good, I kept us on course and we made good speed, probably took a day off our journey. We'll need to head north after midday today. I'm going to rest. Take over, would you?"

"Of course, Captain. Will you speak with your brother?"

I raised an eyebrow. "Is that your business?"

"No, Captain. Sorry. Rest, I'll keep everything going up here."

I clapped him on the back and strode down the steps to my quarters, the tiredness heavy on my shoulders. "Riston, check the ballast, would you? Make sure we're still even after last night."

"Already done, Captain."

"Good man," I said, patting his shoulder as I rounded him to my cabin door.

"Did you want me to fetch you a drink?"

My ears pricked at the words, and my hand longed for the feel of a bottle in them. "No," I answered.

"You can't stop out-right. It should be gradual."

"I don't remember asking your opinion, nor advice, Bo'sun." I said, throwing his position in his face. Clearly, everyone needed a reminder of who I was on this ship.

"Apologies, Captain. I just know what it's like," he said and turned back to face the deck. "Come on, you dogs! Loose those sails! Zandra, Cerys, inspect the ship for any damages from the storm. Step lively!"

I closed the door of my cabin, only slightly blocking out the noise from the deck as the crew scrambled to make sail. I collapsed onto my bed. It was covered in books and charts from before we'd arrived in Isidia. I couldn't be arsed to move them, so I curled around them, the corners of covers and spines pricking my body as I closed my eyes and slept.

I woke to the squawking of gulls echoing through an open window in my cabin. I didn't remember opening it, but eagerly sucked in the fresh air. My mouth felt dry and fuzzy, my face sore from the lines imprinted in it from the scrolls I'd collapsed onto. I rubbed my face and rose from my bed, peeling off my still damp shirt.

"Bellona, Gods!" Peverell exclaimed.

"What the—" I covered myself speedily. "What the fuck is with you and Darius coming into my rooms without knocking?" I complained, shrugging on a robe to cover myself better and turning to face my brother. "What do you want?"

He was sitting in a chair by my desk, fiddling with the map and his notebook. "I wanted to show you what I've translated, and to apologize."

"Did you open my window?" I asked, walking over to it and slamming it shut.

"Yes, it stank like a whorehouse in here."

I laughed. "As if you'd know."

"Can I apologize or what?" he demanded.

I nodded.

"I'm sorry for disrespecting you in front of your crew. I was just worried about you. After seeing how rough you were in Isidia, I wasn't sure if you were right-minded enough to pull something like that off, but you did. And you were right, I am disconnected from the sea and from you."

I shifted uncomfortably. Peverell had always been one to share his feelings openly and apologize first, and I'd never known how to take it.

"You're a great captain, I can see that already after only three days on your ship, and your crew loves you, Jarrell has said as much."

"I suppose I should thank you for apologizing. Forgive me if I don't do the same, I told you what it would be like here and you went against it."

"No, no, you're completely in the right."

I didn't know what else to say, I wasn't used to winning so easily. Had it been Eevan with me, we'd have argued for days, possibly even taken to fighting on the deck. It had happened before, and I'd won. But Peverell made it impossible to stay angry at him, he always had and it had always infuriated me more. "What have you found then?" I asked, avoiding any more talk of apologies and rights and wrongs.

"Well," he said, unfolding the map and opening his notebook, "some of the words don't have direct translations, but basically, it says that a piece of the map can be found in the marked location, and the location should be a shrine. It could be to either the Mother or the Father, but the Shinchaku have changed things in recent years, so it could be a joint shrine to both now." At my bored expression, he sighed and continued, "All of this to say, it's in a shrine and there may be some … difficulties getting to the map piece."

I grinned, my blood rushing through my body with excitement. "What kind of difficulties?"

"Traps and the sort."

"Traps I can handle."

"Are we the only ones with knowledge of this map?"

"As far as I know, yes," I said, sitting on the edge of my desk and pulling my pipe out of a drawer. "Though I don't know much, to be fair."

"I worry about other interested parties."

"Other interested parties I can handle."

My brother pinched the bridge of his nose. "Your overconfidence will be our downfall."

"Or our triumph," I countered, lighting my pipe and drawing the smoke into my mouth. "It's all about how you view it, brother."

"What if this map leads to nothing? What if it's already been found?"

"Then we've just had a good time. Not everything needs to pay off in the end."

Peverell's brows rose. "I suppose that's one way to view it."

"Does your research say anything about what the traps could be?" I asked, leaning over to gaze at his notes.

Peverell waved the smoke from my pipe out of his face and sat back. "Not really, and I can't say I know much about Shinchaku traps outside of this. It's not really anything I've had to research before."

I nodded, racking my brain for any knowledge I could have on the issue. I came up with nothing. "I'll cross the hurdle of traps when we get to it. So far, I've never encountered any I couldn't get through."

"Just you'll be going? Alone?"

I shrugged. "Why risk the life of my crew for my own selfish endeavor?"

He chuckled. "How mature of you. If Islina had seen this side of you, perhaps she would like you better."

"Perhaps." I chewed on the mouthpiece of my pipe, considering the new information. The Shinchaku wouldn't be happy with us sneaking around one of their shrines. The humans still regarded the Mother and Father rather highly, but given the size of the village, I was sure we could get in and out without causing a larger problem. And did I want to venture into the shrine alone? What dangers could I face within if I did? Peverell certainly couldn't come with me, he would only slow me down. I could have Jarrell or Riston accompany me, but I didn't want to leave the rest of the crew with no one to lead them back home. My stomach growled, pulling me from my thoughts. When had I last eaten?

"I'm starved, come eat with me," I said, rising to head to the mess deck.

"I've already eaten, I'm just going to head back to my rooms and see if there's anything else I can get from this before we arrive."

"There'll be heaps of time for that," I said, throwing open the door to the deck, my robe fluttering in the wind. My brows rose as I saw what sat in the distance. "How long was I asleep for?"

"Almost two days," Riston said, coming across the deck to Peverell and I.

"We're almost there then, good show," I said, pushing past them both and heading below deck. I wasn't in the mood for a lecture from Riston, and if we were almost there I needed to eat and get my strength up. Some of the crew were sleeping, swinging peacefully in their hammocks above the cannons, others sat on stools and played cards. I nodded at the few that noticed me and rounded the stairs toward the galley, the smell of bread and freshly butchered meat filling the already stale air.

"Captain," came the gruff voice of our new cook. His pale Isidian skin reflected even the slightest amount of light, as his raven hair seemed to drink it in. "Halen," he said, one hand on his chest, the other holding a bloodied cleaver. "We've not met yet."

"No, how did you come to join my crew?" I said, picking up a loaf of bread, still warm from the oven.

"Jarrell picked me up at the docks in Lonthia. Your old cook was nowhere to be found when the King gave the order to prepare the ship."

"So, Jarrel just hired you on the spot?" I asked, my mouth full of warm, perfectly baked bread.

"Aye, I told him I used to be a cook in the Isidian navy. He said I'd do and put me to work."

"What fortune."

Halen shrugged and hobbled around the butcher's block. "Not a lot of good to the navy like this," he said, shaking his wooden leg, and it was then that I noticed he was missing a few fingers too.

"What happened?" I asked, nodding my thanks as he bought me a flagon of water.

"A skirmish with some Osirians—they were crossin' borders they shouldn't've been." He wiggled the remaining fingers on his right hand, his thumb, middle and little. "They captured me and tortured me, the bastards. Was just lucky I'm left-handed."

"I thought the grudge was forgotten?"

"Isn't your brother the King?" he asked, sounding almost amused at my lack of knowledge.

I shrugged.

"It mostly is, at least we keep our distance. But, when it comes to the sea, the Osirians get a bit lax with borders and agreed upon trade routes."

I was embarrassed, not that Halen had intended it, but this was all stuff I should've known—as a sea captain, the Isidian King's sister, and as a Carracallan. It made me reconsider who really was disconnected from the sea. It had been a long while since I'd sailed for more than pleasure around Carynthia. I mostly stuck to the coast and skipped through towns along the way, seeking pleasure and inebriation wherever I could. "Well, if your bread is always this good, then I'm glad to have you aboard, sir." The cook nodded and went back to chopping the skinned leg of a beast into chunks—for a stew, most likely, that would last for lunch, dinner and probably breakfast. I refilled my flagon and carried it and the bread back up through the deck to my quarters, stopping at the port side of the ship to gaze out at the land coming to shape on the horizon.

Mist covered the mountains, from this distance I couldn't see them, but I knew pines lined the sides of the rocky cliffs as well. It had been many years since I'd been to Shinchaku. I'd been favoring sailing further east to the other elven lands; their strange devices fascinated me, but they were not so welcoming to outsiders—especially not deformed ones such as me. They saw themselves as the Prime Elven race and us as corruptions and traitors. We traded what we could, what little they would accept, and received whatever they would offer. It didn't matter what it was really, anything they gave us was new and advanced, much more than anything we had in Carynthia. They had no magic, but they had something we didn't—works of genius that bewildered even the sharpest of Carynthian minds. Perhaps we would visit there again, once this quest was over with.

I kicked open the door to my rooms and kicked it shut again once I was inside, collapsing into the armchair by the windows and watching the waves as I ate. The bread was a blessing with each bite, the water with every sip. My hands shook less as each bit of sustenance hit my stomach. I held my left hand up to study it, tried my best to hold it still, had it always been this unsteady?

A voice in the back of my mind told me that drink would help, it always helped, we never shook when we were in a state of inebriation. I ignored it. It was wrong. When I was drunk, I always fell over, slurred, and picked fights. I wasn't going to do that anymore. I was going to get sober.

I drank down my flagon of water, slamming the empty vessel down onto my desk. Water was the only drink I needed. Water and tea. I would allow myself tea.

I opened the window I sat before, sucking in the fresh air and letting it fill and cool my cabin. I couldn't tell if the sweat was from the heat or lack of drink and other substances that usually filled my system, but it poured down my back and face in almost a stream. Just a few days and it would pass. Contrary to everyone's beliefs, I had been sober before, for a long period. I knew what to expect and how to deal with it, but that was a long time ago.

I thought of calling Riston to ask him to fetch me a drink, but I would not give in so easily. Soon enough, we would reach the shores of Shinchaku and I wanted to be in my best state of mind to handle that. I hadn't thought of it before, but after Peverell mentioned other interested parties, a weight seemed to sit in my stomach. After all, I didn't know where the Isidian had gotten the map or who he'd told about it. I just had to hope that he'd offered it up because he couldn't read the text—and he probably wanted to fuck me. Thought he could drink me under the table and convince me to leave with him. Many had tried that, many underestimated me. After this, perhaps they would not

CHAPTER 5

We reached Shinchaku two days later, just after dawn, the air already moist and sticky with heat.

"Let's try not to lose anyone at this port," I said to Jarrell as I filled my pack with food, water skins, and rope. "The Shinchaku will not be happy with me breaking into their temple, so we'll need to leave as fast as possible. After I disembark, hang around for a few hours, then head back out. I'll swim or steal a dinghy to get back to you."

"You're going alone?" he asked with a hint of exasperation.

"Yes. I don't want to have to worry about others' safety, or how to return them to the ship. It's faster for me to just swim, if possible."

"I don't know if I like that," he said, cupping his neck with his gray hand.

"It'll be fine." I shoved my tighter swimming clothes into my bag. "Just keep my brother occupied so he's not stressing the whole time I'm gone." He tried to hide it, but from the corner of my eye I saw him perk up at my words. I sighed, I would have to speak to Peverell about that. "If I don't come back after two days, take Peverell back to Isidia. But don't worry, I'll be back," I said with a grin. I closed my bag and swung it onto my back, slapping Jarrell hard on the shoulder as I left the room, ignoring his worried black eyes as they followed me out.

I crossed the deck and headed down to the stateroom, where Peverell was. The gun deck was a mess of crew preparing to make port and probably hoping to visit the nearest brothel. I had strict rules on my ship about sexual relations—you didn't fuck the people you worked with. Simple. And most adhered to it.

When I entered the stateroom, Peverell was sitting by the galley window, staring at the scenic mountain range that surrounded the port village. From his concerned expression, it was clear he already knew what I was here to say.

"You can come to shore for a moment, but then I'd like you back on the ship," I said, looking over his notebook that sat open on the large round table in the center of the room; he'd already begun documenting our journey for Eevan.

"You don't have to do this alone," he said, not taking his eyes from the window.

"I know, it's honestly just easier."

Peverell sighed and pinched the bridge of his nose, running his fingers over his blue eyebrows. "The shrine should be toward the back of the city. You'll have to climb quite a few stairs to reach it, but at least you'll know it when you see it."

"Is that it?"

"There'll be traps, so be careful, and it's just a map piece so it may not be the only treasure in there, but try not to get distracted. And be wary of other parties, we can't be the only ones that know about this."

"Will it just be in the shrine?" I asked. Surely if it was, someone would have found it by now.

"I'm not sure, our map doesn't have a lot of information regarding its true location. You may need to poke around a bit. The only thing I did find that could be a clue is a tiny depiction of a sea serpent but, like I said, I don't know who the shrine is dedicated to now—it could have changed since this map was created."

"Right, so trek up some stairs, look for a sea serpent, dodge the traps, get the map piece. Sounds pretty simple to me." I clapped my hands.

"Bellona, be serious for a moment, please. This could be dangerous," Peverell pleaded, turning to face me. "I don't want to end up returning home only to tell mother and father that you died due to your own stubbornness and immaturity," he snapped.

"Immaturity?" I spat. "I'm going alone for everyone else's safety. Jarrell has a bad shoulder, Riston has a family, as does most of the crew. You'll need them to sail home and, anyway, this is meant to be a stealthy operation. If we get caught, it's a lot easier for one to escape than multiple. And what about you, brother, with your knowledge and"—I looked over his thin form—"nothing else? Books aren't going to help you when you're being chased down a mountain side by armed guards, Peverell, and they're certainly not going to help you swim out of harm's way. What if one of the shrine's traps is to fill with water? Do you have gills?" I made a show of checking his neck. "Hmm, doesn't look like it. And what happened to, 'How mature of you, Bellona, to put your own life before your crew's'?" I said, mimicking his words from two days ago.

"I've had more time to think on it and I think it's suicide," he threw back, his voice rising. "Your gills don't make you immune to death, Bellona."

"Alright, well, I'm going now." Turning to leave, I could hear his heavy foot falls as he stalked across the room to follow me and continue our argument. "I'll be back before you know it," I said, smiling as I slammed the door in his face and turned my skeleton key in the lock, trapping him in the room.

He tried the handle and when the door didn't open, he pounded on it with a fist. "Bellona, open this door!"

"Oops, sorry, it seems I'm too immature." I gave the door a kick. "You can stay in there until I come back! Jarrell will bring you food and drink at meal times, you will not fight him to exit. And no fucking him, either!" I added, remembering the bit of excitement that had settled over Jarrell when I'd asked him to keep an eye on Peverell.

I stalked back through the deck, buttoning my shirt up around my neck to cover my gills and adding a scarf to hold my collar up for good measure as I went; I didn't need the crowd that they always drew. The gangway was just being lowered to the dock as I crossed the main deck. Jarrell stood off to the side, watching the crew as they lowered it and scrambled to the docks to tie off the mooring lines.

"Stick to the plan," I said, readjusting my pack on my shoulders. "Peverell doesn't leave his room." I added, giving Jarrell a stern look.

"Aye, Captain," he said. "Good luck."

I nodded and stepped onto the gangway, running through the plan and Peverell's directions as I made my way through the docks and into town.

The Shinchaku had built their town a little ways back from the shore, as if they were frightened the creatures lurking beneath the depths would come ashore to eat them if they were any closer. By the time I reached the center, I was coated in sweat, my normally flat hair curling at the ends from the moisture in the air and my stomach growling from the scent of food.

Fish and meat hung from wooden awnings and rested in crates along the main road, fresh enough that they didn't smell yet and still left trails of blood flowing down into small trenches dug on either side of the dirt road. Other vendors had crates full of vegetables and fruits, large sacks of rice stacked on top of each other, and both fresh and dried noodles for those wealthy enough to afford to not make their own. I purchased a steamed bun from a baker; inside was a sweet pork filling. It was delicious, but the sweet flavor of the bun and the pork made me long for a bitter ale to wash it down with. I instead purchased a strong green tea, its bitterness almost dispelling the longing I felt.

I was surprised that the streets weren't more busy, even though children ran freely between the market stalls, their wooden shoes clacking against their feet, and a few men and women walked through the streets perusing the stalls and speaking to each other. I turned to the woman running the tea shop, her long dark hair pulled back loosely from her face and fashioned into a knot atop her head.

"Where is everyone?" I asked.

She raised her brown eyes to mine and almost gaped at me. "Fighting."

I looked at her blankly.

"In the war," she said as if I'd been born yesterday.

"What war?" The last time I'd been out in the world there had been peace.

"The Aurali attacked," she said, shifting a container of leaves and putting more water over a fire to boil. "Something about the Sillessians favoring us." She wiped a pink hand over her brow, flicking the sweat to the floor. "There's no truth to it, the Sillessians aren't capable of picking favorites, but now our men and women have to go out to fight."

I shook my head, another war brought on by human selfishness and insecurity. I wondered how long it would be before elves got involved, before the feud between Isidia and Osiria once again bubbled to the surface and caused more destruction. I pinched the bridge of my nose, running my fingers over my brows and massaging my temples. Conflict between the humans brought with it more hassle for me, especially if my father got involved. I just had to hope elves would keep their noses out of this one and let the humans have at it for a while. The last thing I wanted was to have to fight in another war.

I thanked the woman for the tea and rose from my stool.

Stalking through the town and running through the plan in my head, I barely noticed that the townsfolk had retreated into their homes before I came face to face with an Osirian male—that would do it.

His white hair was neatly pulled back from his face in a low ponytail that shone in the summer sun, his violet skin stained pinkish on his cheeks from being in the heat too long, form hidden by long robes. His amber eyes fell on me and widened.

He stopped a distance away. "Afternoon, are you comfortable with me coming nearer?" he asked in a friendly tone. Most Osirians followed the same protocol before approaching people.

"I have no fear of you, Deathbringer," I said, eyeing him suspiciously. It wasn't odd to run into other elves while on the road, but Osirians didn't usually travel this far south.

The Osirian hitched his pack higher on his shoulder and approached me slowly, not reacting at all to the unfavorable name I'd called him. I could tell by the straining in his thin arms that it was quite heavy.

"I'm a scholar from Minoma, studying the temple on the side of that mountain. What a fortuitous circumstance to meet a Carracallan while studying a sea temple," he mused.

"It's a sea temple, then? I haven't made my way up there yet." Had they always taken Osirians at the mage college? I supposed they couldn't say no, though part of me doubted it.

"Oh, yes. It was a temple to the Mother once, but they've since restored it to its original purpose. After all, it is a coastal town, makes more sense to worship the sea than the pit."

"S'pose I have to agree."

The Osirian held out a purple hand. "Helio Lothar, aspiring mage."

I took it and shook it. "Bellona Glenon."

Helio gaped. "My, my, fortuitous indeed! I've long been curious about your gills, though I'm sure everyone is."

"To a degree, yes. Are you headed to the temple now?" I asked, changing the subject, no longer wanting to bask in the glory of my gills after the dressing down I'd received from my brother.

"Well, I was hoping to buy some food first but"—he motioned around us at the empty street—"I'm sure you can see my predicament."

"You cannot hunt? Or fish?"

"More of a scholarly type," he admitted sheepishly.

I pulled some dried meat out of my pack and passed it to him. "Food, in exchange for a tour of the temple?"

He seemed taken aback at first—it could possibly have been the first kind gesture he'd ever received from an outsider.

"Of course," he said, taking the meat and leading me to the edge of the mountain side. I watched him warily as he downed the meat while we walked, almost choking he was eating it so fast. It was odd to have run into him, but perhaps it was just fortune. If he was a competitor, I would get as much information as I could from him, then slit his throat before he could even think to raise that curse they called a power.

The trek up the stairs to the temple was torturous—both Helio and I were practically crawling by the halfway point. I'd taken on his pack as well as my own, fed up with him falling behind because of its weight. It was indeed full of books and scrolls, further cementing that he was truly a mage, but part of me was still suspicious.

When we started our trek, he'd explained to me that he'd always been fascinated by the sea, had wanted to learn everything he could about it. So, after the sudden death of his parents, he'd traveled to Minoma and began studying. He could have learned magic in Osiria, but he didn't much care for the Phoenix Priestesses that ran the college there. "Terrible women. They hate humans, never believed they should have magic as they do. I could ignore it if it were just something they talked about every so often, but they force the belief on you—and the King can do nothing, not when his wife is one of them," he spat.

"So you went completely against them and studied magic with humans?" I laughed.

"Seemed the right way to atone for my king's foolishness."

"I wouldn't have thought the humans would accept you," I stated bluntly.

Helio's face turned grim. "It took a long time, a long, painful time, but they came around. The Arch-Mage once vowed he'd never turn away a willing student, and I used this vow to my advantage."

"As any cunning scholar would."

"And what of you, Princess? What brings you to this small village in Shinchaku?"

"Curiosity, I haven't been here in"—I thought for a moment, counting on my fingers—"well, almost a decade. Thought it was about time I ventured back."

He questioned me no more after that and we'd fallen into a long silence.

Now, we were collapsed at the midway point, guzzling water, and I wiped sweat from my face with an envious look at Helio—the scholar panted but not a bead fell from his brow. Oh, to be Osirian, if only for the sweat free summers.

"We're close," he said between breaths. "We'll make it before the afternoon."

"How often do the people come here to pray?" I huffed out.

"Almost every day, if not multiple times a day."

"No wonder the children in town have so much energy." I shielded my eyes and gazed down the mountainside to the sea; I could see *The Siren* bobbing in the bay, awaiting my return.

I pulled some dried meat from my bag and gnawed on it, offering some to the Osirian beside me.

He declined it.

I studied his face as he gazed toward our final destination at the height of the stairs. His nose was straight, his eyes large and round, shining gold in the midday sun, lips pulled thin in thought. I wondered if we'd have time to stop at a tavern before night fell.

"What's your plan after you see the shrine?" I asked, leaning back on the stairs behind me and sticking out my chest, tilting my head back as if to soak up the sun. I watched out of the side of my eye as Helio's eyes raked up my body.

"Well, I suppose I'll return to my campsite—it's just outside town."

"You're not staying in town?" I regretted the words the second they'd passed through my lips.

Helio's face fell. "No." Was all he said.

"Apologies, I didn't think."

"It's fine. It's not the norm for everyone. Decades ago, people were too fearful to turn us away, though they wanted to. So, in a way, this is an improvement."

"Humans," I spat. "They fear everything, anything that is different from them. It's pathetic."

"You are not afraid? Many elves are."

"I am not. I've faced Osirians in battle before—if you'd wanted to kill me, you'd have done it by now. "

Helio laughed. "The words of an adventurer."

"The words of someone with sense." I rose and hauled my pack onto my shoulders. "Let's continue before it gets too late."

The scholar nodded and we proceeded to struggle up the steps, our legs shaking and lungs burning. I prayed that the temple above was worth this pain, that the treasure was worth it.

CHAPTER
6

I was strong, no one would deny that, but the climb up the stairs showed me that my lungs were weak. My legs were good in short sprints, but the height of the stairs, the steepness, had them at their limits—there was no way I was going to walk all the way back to town just to come back up later tonight. I'd have to figure out a way to ditch the Osirian and find somewhere in the mountains to hide out during the day.

As we climbed the last of the steep stairs, the temple came into view, its red and gold paint beaming in the full sun. The sloped roof rising at the corners and pointing upward to the sky, to the Father, the god the Shinchaku associated with water. Thick wooden pillars and beams made up the bulk of the structure and as we topped the last step I spied an altar made from a large block of blue crystal, scenes of ancient voyagers and great sea monsters carved delicately into each side.

Troughs of water sat outside the temple to wash in, with large ladles resting on wooden hooks for scooping the water and running it over your hands. I felt a sudden rush of shame for not knowing if it was customary at all shrines or just this particular one. For the fire shrine, did you have to run your hands through a live flame?

I mimicked the Osirian as he prepared to enter under the large red gate of the temple, washing my hands and removing my boots and socks, placing them beside the other discarded shoes neatly lined along the stone wall that encompassed the shrine site. Behind the altar was a large painting of the Father, done in the traditional Shinchaku style of brush and ink on a thick scroll. He looked fierce, his face—verging on demonic—resembled the monstrous creatures he let roam his seas. He was depicted standing in the center of a swirling maelstrom, the competing currents shown as inky spirals surrounding his terrifying figure. While it was not the way the Carracallans viewed the Father, I appreciated the skill of the artist. The feelings of dread and admiration the image summoned within me were certainly real.

I kept to the edge of the temple, leaving the few Shinchaku to their prayers as I scouted the area. There were no guards, why would there be? The few patrons there were seemed to simply pray and leave, and the stream of worshipers was dying down the later it got. Many would need to begin preparing for the end of the day. It wouldn't be long before there was no one else there but me and the Osirian. I scanned the temple for him, expecting to see him curled in a corner writing down every little detail he could about the place, as Peverell would have insisted on doing, but his bag had been discarded by the door and he was nowhere in sight.

I stalked from the temple and walked the outer perimeter, scanning for Helio. Pine trees surrounded the grounds of the temple, and other trees I didn't know the names of, but they added a nice leafy contrast. Large stones and other small, maintained bushes lined pathways that wove through the yard, and I could hear the tinkling sound of a water feature nearby. I predicted that the water must be coming from an underground stream, most likely from ice melting on the tops of the mountains. I rounded the northern edge of the shrine and found Helio squatting by a wall, wiping his sleeve on the wall to dislodge caked dirt. He was so engrossed in his work that he didn't notice me. I leaned against the wall, arms crossed over my chest, and cleared my throat.

Helio jumped, almost falling back on his arse. "Highness, you frightened me."

"What are you doing back here?" I asked, pushing off the wall and walking toward him.

He rose to meet my height. "I was just examining the outside of the temple. The Shinchaku are known to carve messages or signatures into their buildings."

"Uh-huh, and are you looking for one in particular?"

"Now, why would you ask that, Princess?" His voice seemed to shift with the words, into one deeper and challenging.

I stepped closer, rising to the challenge. "Answer the question, mage."

The reminder of his place seemed to snap the sense back into him. "I am. The signature of the original builder of the temple. Their name has been lost in time, I'm hoping to discover it."

I looked him over. He seemed to be slender beneath his robes, but they could be hiding toned muscle. I was making my suspicions clear, hoping to discourage the Osirian. If it came to blows, I would win—I was almost double his size. And if he used his cursed power, he'd have the whole of Carracalla and Isidia up his arse.

"You must have a brilliant memory to not need to consult your books," I observed, nudging my head toward the doorway of the shrine.

He grinned. "I can remember whole pages after only seeing them once, the Arch-Mage says it's a blessing, a sign that I was meant to study. I can retrieve my books if it would make you more comfortable," he added mockingly.

I waved him off and stalked back inside the temple to examine the altar. The mage was bullshitting, I knew it, it was practically wafting off him like a stench.

The last of the Shinchaku had left the temple and were heading back down toward the steps, giving me the ability to freely wander. I climbed the steps to the altar and studied the carvings; they were so detailed I hardly believed they could have been carved by the hands of a human. To elves, they seemed so slow and clumsy, but clearly there were some out there with steady enough hands to rival even the most talented elven artisans.

I studied the scenes carved into the crystal face and couldn't find the sea serpent for the life of me, but it showed every other monstrous sea beast I'd had the pleasure of meeting. The kraken that haunted the seas off the Carracallan coast that had an appetite for dogs—if you weren't careful, she'd reach up and snatch them right off the deck. The creature we called the sea wraith that hung around the waters off the western Osirian coast; it was elusive, could flatten its spine and webbed body until it was practically invisible beneath the waves, it moved with the currents like a piece of seaweed. In the carving, the sea wraith was depicted as drinking blood from the necks of sailors. I'd never experienced this, but I seemed to have an unspoken understanding with all the monsters of the sea.

On the third side was the large lantern beast, named for the light that hung over its huge face from a barb of flesh. When it rose from the seas at night with its lantern out, it looked like nothing more than an approaching ship, and you wouldn't know it was anything other until you were already in its belly, ship and all. And the last was a creature with the tail and body of a fish, but a head almost like a human, with a horn protruding from the front and a large gaping mouth. This particular beast was known to spear ships with its horn and follow them as they took on water and sunk, picking the sailors from the water once it was too late for them to save themselves. But no sea serpent.

I let out a frustrated breath and stalked about the temple, looking for anything that even slightly resembled the serpent. I ducked behind curtains and found rooms of spare ladles, forgotten shoes, and small wooden prayer tokens. I found nothing, in other words.

My vision blurred as I wiped a bead of sweat from my brow, and as it did, I noticed something out of the corner of my eye. A blue serpent.

My eyes flicked to the altar again, but I kept my feet planted firmly where they were. All I saw now was the wraith draining victims of blood and the tail of the lantern beast; but, when I squinted, the ships and lines of victims formed a serpentine body, the wraith the head and the beast its tail. Had I not stood in this exact spot, I never would have spotted it. Clever humans.

Now that I knew where the serpent was, I could leave and hide somewhere until nightfall, then come back to investigate further when there were no more watchful eyes.

"I'm going to head back down to the village," I said to the mage when he re-entered the temple, the sleeves of his robe coated in dirt. "That trek took more out of me than I thought it would. Did you find your signature?"

"No, I didn't," he said, disappointed. "I may come back in the morning, it's getting too dark outside now."

Damn. "Will you walk down with me?" I asked casually.

"I may stay here a little longer, if you don't mind traveling alone. I want to get my notes down while they're fresh in my mind."

Yes! "I don't mind. Perhaps I'll see you in the village later," I said, giving him a wink and sauntering to the stairs. The echoing sound of a dropped quill was my only indication that he'd understood my meaning.

I walked down the first flight of stairs, making sure I was out of sight from the temple before I climbed a nearby pine, the dense branches hiding my presence from anyone above or below, and waited.

After an hour or so, the mage left. I watched him walk down the stairs, eyeing him suspiciously until he was out of view, and then waited a few hours more. Once the village below was dark and I was certain there was no risk of someone coming up to find me poking around, I dropped from the tree.

CHAPTER
7

The temple was silent, barely lit by a streak of moonlight that shone through the open archway, hitting the blue crystal altar and refracting through the temple. I walked around the altar until I found the sweet spot, the sea serpent shape now glaringly obvious in the glow of moonlight. I stared at it for a moment, running through what it could mean in my head before I began poking at the altar, the poking turning more and more violent after a long moment of no reaction.

"Fuck." I sighed, slipping down to the ground beside the altar in defeat. I'd found nothing during the day that could be a lever to a secret door or a false wall—poking at the altar and looking for switches or buttons had been my last idea.

Despite the lateness and lack of sun, the air was still hot and humid. Sweat trickled down my face and back from the walk back up the hill and the stress of not knowing what to do. My fingers ached for the neck of a bottle, the stem of a pipe. I always had better ideas when I was intoxicated, and I sweated less— or was I usually just so far gone that I didn't feel the discomfort?

I leaned my head back against the cool stone of the altar and sighed as a pleasant breeze brushed up my neck.

It took me longer than it should have to realize, my mind distracted by the thoughts of wine and smoke, but eventually, I shot up, my fingers tracing the base of the crystal. Cool air seeped through a tiny gap at the base of the altar. I rose to my feet, braced my hands on the side of the stone, and gave an almighty push, my shoulders instantly burning at the sudden exertion.

The crystal begrudgingly shifted, the base of it grinding on the stone floor of the temple. I prayed the sound would not travel down to the village. I didn't pause to relish in my success when beneath the crystal was a wooden staircase. Instead, I tentatively placed a foot on the first step to test its stability and, when I didn't fall through it to my death, I continued cautiously down the steps.

The air was cool but thick with dust, the staircase pitch black. I wished I'd thought to bring a torch with me, but given the risk of traps, it was better I hadn't. I'd heard stories of other adventurers lighting torches, only to have them explode because of dust traps. Over time, my eyes adjusted as best they could to the dark before a glow appeared at the base, accompanied by a pit-awful smell. I pinched my nose as I reached it, walking under the crudely carved stone archway and into a vast cavern.

The space was a hollowed-out extension of the temple above, the walls that encompassed the domed room were carved with giant depictions of the various sea monsters from the waters around Carynthia, almost scaled to their true sizes. It was unnerving to have their blank eyes staring down at me from the tops of the walls. While ferocious, some of these monsters were creatures I knew, friends even. In the center of the domed ceiling hung a carved-stone chandelier. I didn't know what substance was in there, but whatever it was, it lit the space with a greenish glow.

At the other end of the room was a door painted the same red as the pillars and roof frame of the temple above, but the rest of the large space was empty— save for the corpses that littered the floor. Each corpse was at a different level of decay; some barely had any flesh left, while others looked relatively fresh. That explained the smell.

I took a deep breath and studied the room from my safe distance. What had killed these people? I could see nothing at first that would explain their deaths, until I studied one of the bodies closest to me and saw tiny darts poking from the side of their head and arms. Then, looking at the floor, I noticed a subtle pattern. Every other stone slab had a small, blue speck on it. From a distance, I could only guess it was made of the same crystal as the altar.

Following the trail the blue specks formed across the floor with my eyes, I could see that it made a path to the other side. One would think that should make the journey easy but, no, the slabs with crystals embedded were spread further apart than anyone could easily step between, even elves with our slight height advantage over humans. From my spot by the archway, I could see the first section of the path, but beyond that was obscured, either because of a corpse or the thick dust that had settled on the floor over the thousands of years that this temple had been hidden. No one had ever managed to pass even this first test, it seemed. Whoever had built this trap, this temple, had not intended for the map pieces to ever be claimed, that much was clear.

I took a small knife from my boot and cut the straps on my bag so I could tie it more securely to my person. The last thing I needed was for it to slip off my shoulders and set off the trap. I then double-checked that I was not at risk of items falling from it if I needed to leap between slabs, doing a few test jumps on the spot, stretching my muscles at the same time. Not only would I have to leap between slabs, but I would have to move corpses out of the way at the same time. There was no way I could cross the floor without setting off the traps, so I had to be prepared to deal with that added risk.

I let out a breath and stepped onto the first slab, flinging my arms around my head in the off chance I was wrong. I wasn't, they came away pain and dart free. I sighed and continued on, leaping to the next slab and the next, and the next.

I was a third of the way through the room when I came to my first issue. A corpse lay half on a safe slab and half on one that could kill me. I paused for a moment, thinking of how to proceed, cursing myself for not testing the sensitivity of the floor before leaping across it like an arse. If I leapt and landed on the wrong part of the corpse, it could activate the traps, or it could not. I could also leap across and trip on the corpse, causing me to then activate the traps myself.

I had to risk it, there was no other way.

I bounced on my feet, preparing to make the leap, judging how much force to put into it so that I would land on the far side of the safe slab. I aimed for the crystal, the small blue speck on the corner of the stone.

I was about to jump, my right leg hovering in the air before me ready for the leap, when a cough echoed through the space, causing me to stall. I lost my balance, my arms flailing to keep myself upright without having anything to grab onto.

"Fuck, fuck, fuck!" I leaned back to counter my forward momentum and flapped my arms until I was still.

"Shit! Sorry!"

I turned, knife pulled, and glared at the source of the voice. "What the fuck are you doing here?" I spat.

Helio flung his arms wide. "I could ask you the same thing, Princess." His voice took the same tone it had when I'd confronted him earlier today.

"Oh, fuck off. I knew there was something suspicious about you. Well, here's your perfect chance to kill me." I said, mimicking his wide-armed stance.

"And why would I do that, when it would also kill me?" he said, stepping onto the first of the safe stone slabs. "If you set one slab off, all the statues fire poisonous darts, not just one. It's a clever trap," he said, skipping to the next stone. "I was trying to research what poison they used so I could find an antidote, but alas, they never recorded it." He leapt to the next slab, and the one after that.

"So, you knew I was here for the map piece the whole time?" I asked, watching him come closer and closer to me.

"I had my suspicions."

He was getting too close for my liking. I turned from him and made my leap. I landed on top of the gem, on the toes of my right foot. My pack made me slightly top-heavy. I made to put my left foot down and flinched as it touched the corpse, relaxing when the room didn't explode into chaos.

"Fuck, Bellona. You need to be careful." Helio huffed. "My life is also on the line."

"Like I give a shit about you," I shot back, leaping again to the next step in the path.

I slipped, and my foot skidded past the gem, hitting the tile beside it. A hiss sounded through the room and I heard Helio gasp.

Without thinking twice, I fell to the floor and pulled a corpse atop me. The smell was suffocating, rotten and foul—it was one of the fresh ones. The body shuddered and squelched above me as it was pelted by darts flying through the room in all directions. Gagging, I did my best to stay still, praying there was enough flesh left on the dead body to shield me from the darts.

Then as quickly as it had begun, the barrage stopped. Another hiss sounded through the room and when I poked my head out from under my corpse shield I saw that the eyes and mouths of the statues had opened, revealing the mechanism from which the darts were shot. As I watched, I pushed the tile next to me.

Nothing happened.

The mechanism was too slow to react to new movement, the builders not expecting anyone to survive the first attack. I rose to my feet and bolted—it was only a matter of time before it caught up again.

"Bellona, get down!" Helio yelled.

I ignored him and continued running, my legs burning from the stairs, and my shoulders burning from moving the altar. Each movement I made was laced with a touch of pain.

I pushed my legs to move faster as the hiss once again echoed through the chamber, panic filling my already straining chest. I was so close to the other side, I could see the flat stone that marked the edge of the trapped floor, it was tunneled in my vision. I didn't risk a glance behind me to see if the Osirian was following, or if he was dead. That was his problem. I just kept running, the hiss growing louder and louder in my thundering ears. There was a click of the new darts securing into the firing mechanism and, instead of watching, of knowing, I closed my eyes.

I ran blindly, leaving my fate a mystery even to myself.

There was a sharp pop of air and I knew it was the darts being released again. I flinched and went to raise my arms to cover my head in a futile attempt to save myself when my face collided with the wooden door.

"Fuck!" I gasped as blood poured from my nostrils, the pain shooting through my entire face making my eyes water and restricting my breathing to only my mouth. But I was alive—not an elven pin cushion.

I finally risked the look back, watching the darts shoot through the room. Helio was still on the same tile, hiding under a body as I had, his leather satchel held firmly over his head.

I didn't wait for the darts to stop to see if he would make it out alive—or to confirm his death—I pushed the door open and closed it behind me, praying that he would not follow.

CHAPTER

8

The next chamber was smaller, but in no way easier to navigate. The roof was lower and laced with roots from the trees above, the same chandelier as the other chamber hung in this room on a smaller scale, the light snaking between the roots and making them look as if they were moving.

I made sure to study the floor and walls closely before proceeding. It looked to be just a straightforward hallway, there were no defining features to any of the floor tiles, so I cautiously stepped forward—then the first pit came into view. It was wide and deep, deep enough that the bottom was shrouded in shadow. I suspected that spikes were somehow involved.

The first pit was easy enough for me to jump over, my mother having blessed me with her long legs and height. The second was trickier. It felt as if the creators of the temple wanted it to be found by elves, but they wanted us to work for it. And work I would.

I was most of the way through the room when the doors behind me opened. I was resting, half bent over with my hands on my knees, dried blood caked above my top lip.

"I thought you were dead," I shot across the room.

"Not yet, but you gave it a good go," Helio said between puffed breaths. He must have used my same trick.

I gave up on my resting and kept leaping forward, pushing off the wall when I needed the extra *oomph* to get over the pit.

"How do you have so much energy?" Helio whined.

I ignored him and continued on, determined to beat him to the map piece. The last few pits were too wide for me to jump, even pushing off the wall wouldn't help me get across. I pulled the length of rope from my bag and looked for anything that I could loop it through. The light was dim at the edges of the room, but I could see the roots hanging low. There was one perfectly in the middle, at the very end of the room.

I can throw that far, I thought, *I just need to weigh the end.* I dug through my bag, looking for anything heavy to weigh down the end of the rope. I hadn't thought to bring a grappling hook with me and cursed myself for it. Everything else I had either wasn't heavy enough, or was too small, or too large. In the end, I removed my boot and tied it to the end of the rope. *Gods, I hope this works.*

I heard a scuffle behind me and looked back to see Helio making his first leap across one of the pits.

Shit.

I gave the rope a few test swings, feeling for the weight, then made the first shot. It was under, but not by much. I raced to pull the rope back, the sounds of Helio jumping over the pits ringing in my ears. I threw the boot again, it grazed the ceiling and hit the root, thudding to the floor.

Fuck! I reeled it back in once more. *Third time's the charm!*

I tossed it, under arm, praying to the Father that it would at least hit the ceiling and bounce through the root. It sailed through the air and slipped perfectly through the hooped root.

"Yes!" I looked behind. Helio was at the first of the larger pits. He looked to be deep in thought about how to cross it, and was also nursing a stitch in his side by the way he held his ribs. I laughed as I slacked the rope and swung it behind the boot then again back over the front, creating a loose knot. Then I gripped the rope tightly—wrapping it around one foot and clamping it down with the other—and swung.

It was exhilarating, freeing, being weightless in the air over pits that could cause my death in mere seconds, and then it was just shit.

My toes touched the edge of the last pit and the root began to groan under my weight. *Fuck.* I tried desperately to push my hips forward, but that only made my feet fall out from beneath me. I gripped the rope tighter and prepared myself for the pain I knew was coming. I couldn't hold in the yelp of pain as my hips slammed on the edge of the pit, the stone pinching the skin between it and my bone. It was more painful than I'd imagined, and for a moment, I almost let go of the rope, but I somehow managed to keep hold of it and pull myself up just as the groaning of the root became a snapping. At least Helio would struggle to follow me.

I pulled myself up over the edge of the pit and lay on the floor for a moment, catching my breath and waiting for a little of the pain to subside before continuing on. I flinched and hissed as I prodded my hips; looking down, I could already see a deep bruise, my gray skin now stained black. I wouldn't be surprised if there was some damage to the bone.

Helio was struggling to catch up. He was shorter than me and was already having to think of creative ways to get through the hallway. I pulled myself up, there was no time for healing, it would take too long. I took a deep breath and continued through to the next room of the temple.

I froze in the doorway as I entered, my foot half raised for access to my knife. Before me was a large sea serpent, the same one shown on the altar above.

For a moment, I feared it was alive, but as I looked more carefully, I realized it was indeed made of stone. Cautiously, I entered the room. It was as large as the first, the serpent wrapped around the perimeter and at the center sat a plinth.

This is it. Excitement filled my battered body as I limped to the plinth, my eyes still darting around the room to be sure I was safe from more traps. My hips ached with each movement, the pain throbbing down through my legs. For good measure, I pulled the knife from my boot, ready for anything that might pop up the second I reached the pedestal. But nothing happened when I reached it, because nothing was there.

"No." I groaned. "No, no, no!" I angrily kicked the plinth. Pain shot up my legs and into my bruised hips. "Ah, fuck!" I yelled, doubling over.

"I have to say, I am very impressed, Princess," said a cool voice behind me.

I groaned again and tightened my grip on my knife. "I could say the same about you if I weren't so disappointed that you're still breathing."

Helio laughed. "I suppose that's fair." His slow steps echoed through the chamber. "Isn't it beautiful? You'd never expect something like this to be made by the hands of humans." He stopped walking a few steps from me. "And the traps, so clever. They really didn't want anyone finding this treasure. From my readings, I gather that the original builders were so determined to keep this place secret that they sacrificed themselves in the very pits we just crossed. What admirable diligence."

"Well, it was for naught. The treasure is gone—they were fools." I spat, rising to my feet. "And you knew it was gone, so why lead me on this bullshit chase?"

"I wanted to see if you could handle it, because I need your help."

"You have it, don't you?" I asked, not really needing an answer, I could see it in his eyes. "That's fine, I'll just kill you for it."

I charged at him, knife raised.

He blocked with his bag, pushing me to the side and then swinging at my head with the satchel. I rolled away, landing on my feet in seconds—enough time to grip the bag and rip it from his grasp. He stumbled and I stabbed my knife through his arm. He let out a cry of pain and fell backwards, blood pooling on the ground around him.

I ripped open the satchel and poured out the contents. "No." I ground out as I dug through the ink-stained pages. "You fucking idiot!"

I'd found the map piece—it was completely destroyed. Ink spread across the page, staining the whole thing black. I tossed it to the floor and threw myself on top of Helio, my hands around his neck. "Why would you have a bottle of ink in a bag with a map?!" I screamed at him, pushing my thumbs against his throat.

He writhed beneath me. "You can't kill me!" He gasped. "I know where the last piece is."

I loosened my hands, but kept them firmly around his neck. "Where?"

"Keep me alive—take me to your ship and I'll tell you where to go," he said hoarsely.

I stared into his eyes, looking for any hint of a lie. They stared right back, challenging but desperate. If he wanted me dead, he would have done it by now.

He needed me, for what I didn't know, but it was keeping me alive as much as it was keeping him alive. I sat back on his hips. "If you're lying to me, you're dead. If you fuck with my crew, you're dead. And if you screw me over—"

"I'm dead, I get it," he said, his voice like gravel.

I stood and swung my leg over him to walk away, kicking him in the head in the process. "*Oops*, sorry," I said with false sheepishness.

He groaned and rose to his feet. "For the record, you could have killed me and stolen the map if you hadn't set off the dart trap in the other room."

"Shut up," I shot back at him, leaving the room with him trailing behind me.

CHAPTER

9

I healed my hips as we sneaked down the mountain, sticking to the treeline to hide from any early rising Shinchaku. Helio stayed close to my side, as if worried I was going to leave him to get caught by the villagers. All was going smoothly until we reached the base of the path.

Two warriors stood there with the woman from the tea shop.

"They never came down," she insisted. "They've broken into the temple, I'm sure of it."

"Then they are dead," one of the warriors said dismissively, his hand resting on the hilt of his long Shinchaku blade.

A chill ran down my spine. I hadn't been worried because I'd thought this village was too small for warriors of his like. I'd figured the most I'd run into would be village guards, not full-on Shinchaku swordsmen.

"This is bad," I whispered to Helio.

If we were caught by the swordsmen, we were dead. They were better trained, their weapons better made, than any others in Carynthia.

"I doubt it. The Osirian's been sniffing around for a week, and the Carracallan … I can't be sure, but I think it's the Princess."

Fuck …

"Hmm, that could mean trouble," the female warrior chimed. "Especially if the Princess has perished. The last thing we need is a war with the Carracallans."

The first warrior sighed. "Fine, we'll head up and investigate."

I let out a breath of relief and waited for the warriors to pass us before turning to Helio and motioning for him to walk behind the line of houses, carefully. But as I moved to follow him, my foot slipped and crunched on a fallen pine branch. My back straightened when my ears caught the quiet *shing* of a blade being drawn.

Run, I mouthed silently to Helio.

We bolted.

I made sure to cover my gills as we ran. I didn't want them to confirm the shop woman's suspicions and drag my family further into this mess. We probably could have explained our way out of trouble, but it wasn't worth the hassle. If I didn't make it back to the ship tonight, they'd leave without me, and if the Shinchaku found out that Helio and I had stolen and ruined their map piece they'd most likely kill us and start a war with Carracalla, Isidia, and Osiria—and my life wasn't worth all that.

I knew we were being followed, but our pursuers were so light on their feet it made it impossible to judge how close they were by sound alone. Elves were faster than humans, but the blades the Shinchaku used were long and fiercely sharp. I risked a look behind and managed to quickly duck as said blade swiped for my neck.

"Shit." I gasped. "Run faster!" I called to Helio.

He pushed his legs faster, his pack seemingly not causing him the same grief as it had earlier.

Bastard.

"Stop!" One of the warriors called.

I responded by flinging a small knife over my shoulder. It clinked against one of the warriors' blades as they deflected it, and I threw another, hoping it was distraction enough.

"Where are we going?" Helio yelled over his shoulder, thankfully not slowing his pace.

"Into the drink!" I called back, trailing him as he redirected toward the docks.

It was still early, too early, I would have thought, for dockworkers to be up, but they were. Humans littered the dock, readying small finishing boats and fixing nets along the jetties.

The dockworkers hopped out of the way as we darted past them, the swordsmen hot on our heels. I hissed as a dart shot past my face, leaving a sting across my cheek. Warm blood trickled down my neck.

Fuck.

I pushed my legs to move faster, grabbing Helio's hand as I sprinted past him and pulled him along behind me, practically dragging him.

More darts flew past us, some narrowly missing, others skimming our arms and legs, leaving small wounds. When a dart struck me full in the shoulder, I decided that we wouldn't make it the whole length of the jetty and pushed Helio into the water, diving in after him myself.

The water was cold and dark, but it took me no time to spot Helio in the deep shadows of the jetty, his white hair a beacon in the gloom. I swam over to him, untying the scarf from my neck and wrapping it around the Osirians head. He looked confused for a moment, but soon seemed to grasp why I'd done it. He gestured upward with his hands, then wrapped them around his neck.

Air. He hadn't had a chance to hold his breath before I'd lurched him into the water.

Shaking my head, I gestured to my mouth, then to his. When he tilted his head to the side in confusion, I rolled my eyes and pulled him toward me, forcing my mouth onto his, parting his lips with my tongue and blowing out the air from my lungs and into his. I pulled away, and after he gestured that he was alright, led him through the water.

I was running on the hope that the Shinchaku wouldn't take to their boats and hunt us further, that perhaps they'd just think we were two stupid, runaway kids. Humans never could tell the ages of elves, even though, to us, it was obvious. Young elves had brighter eyes, stronger figures and magic, held ourselves taller than older elves. It was subtle, too subtle for humans to notice.

When I deemed it safe enough, Helio and I rose to the surface of the water and I glanced back to the shore. The swordsmen seemed to have given up the chase—they were probably halfway up the mountain to inspect what we'd been up to—and I couldn't spot anyone else trailing us, the sun now mostly risen over the horizon. We had made sure to replace the altar to its original position, and I prayed that that would be enough to deter them from pursuing us. They certainly wouldn't make it through the traps, not if even elves struggled.

Helio sucked in air as if it were his first time breathing, but he held himself well enough above the water.

"You can swim?" I asked. It wasn't a normal skill to have, even among sailors. Many overestimated the build of their vessels.

"Yes," he breathed. "Though I won't be able to forever, so if we could carry on."

I rolled my eyes and directed him toward *The Siren* before slipping under the water and swimming there as fast as possible. When dealing with Osirians, it was always better to give warning. Not that my crew particularly cared who you were or where you were from, but caution should be taken around those who control death.

I pulled myself onto the deck of the ship, panting slightly at the distance of the swim and yanking the dart from my shoulder.

"Captain!" One of the carpenters exclaimed, helping me rise.

"Thank you …" I paused, not remembering which of the twins she was.

"Cerys," she said with an understanding smile. They were identical, apart from a small blemish on one of their rears, apparently.

"Captain! What happened?" Jarrell asked, darting across the deck.

"Traps, swordsmen, the usual," I said, sleeking my hair back from my face, "and I picked up a friend along the way." I jerked my thumb over my shoulder to the water.

Jarrell squinted at the waves, his eyes widening as he spotted the Dark-Elf bobbing through the waves toward us. "And what were they doing here?"

"After the same thing we were, but got to it first." I nodded thanks as I accepted a tankard of water from Riston. "He destroyed the map to have his life spared. Be wary."

Jarrell and Riston shared a look, confirming with each other that they knew the orders.

I crossed the deck, ready to collapse in my quarters, when another thought occurred to me. "When our *friend* gets on board, send him to my cabin."

"Captain, your brother—"

"Knows how to pick a lock," Peverell cut in from the doorway of my room.

"Well done, brother, perhaps there's hope for you yet," I said, pushing past him.

"I want to speak to you," he demanded.

"And I want to change," I shot back.

"I'll face the corner and close my eyes."

"Fine," I conceded.

Peverell slammed the door and moved to the corner, turning his back to me. "I'm furious with you, Bellona. What you did yesterday was reckless and stupid ..."

"Yes, *father*." I murmured and ignored Peverell as I undressed, dried myself, and redressed while he prattled on. Eevan wouldn't have done this. Sure, he'd have argued with me before I left, but he'd have celebrated my return, not chastised me for it.

"... then Riston joined us and fucked Zandra from behind—"

"Wait, what?!"

"You weren't even listening to me, were you?"

"Look, I don't need you to discipline me, Pev. I know what I'm doing. My crew trusts me, they know what I can handle and when I'm being too confident."

"And I don't?" His tone was equal parts accusatory and apologetic.

"No, you don't."

His shoulders fell.

I sighed. "You haven't been to sea with me before, you couldn't know."

"But Eevan has," he said, his tone shifting to defeat. "You wish he'd come, don't you?"

"Eev and I just get along better, we always have." I moved to my desk, the sound of my chair scraping along the floor signaling that it was all right for him to turn around. "You and Darius were always closer."

Peverell snorted. "Darius used me to pass his exams and write his proposals. He doesn't—we're not close, not like you and Eevan."

"You think Eevan and I never used each other?" I laughed, slouching down in my chair and lifting my legs to rest my feet on the desk. "Half the blood stains on the deck are the aftermath of Eevan and me using each other. That's life," I added with a shrug.

"And now you're both using me," he concluded.

My gut pinched in an unfamiliar way. "I wouldn't put it that way."

The door to my cabin crashed open and a sopping-wet Osirian stumbled in. "What the—"

"Prince Peverell, would you give my friend and me some privacy, please?" I said.

Pev hesitated for a moment, looking between me and Helio, before deciding against inciting another argument and slamming the door as he left.

CHAPTER

10

Helio collapsed into the chair across from me, his breathing coming fast and ragged. He'd shed his robe, now in a soaked shirt and pants that he must've been wearing beneath. They clung to his lithe form and dripped on my floors.

"I thought you would at least send a boat out," he whined, unwrapping my scarf from around his wrist and throwing it to the floor.

"You thought wrong." I shrugged, crossing my hands over my chest and leaning further back in my chair.

"And had I drowned?"

"My crew would have retrieved you before that."

His amber eyes sparked, his mouth setting itself into a thin line as he wrestled against a rebuke.

"So, where to?" I asked, indicating the map spread out on the desk under my heels.

"Right to business, ey?"

"No point fucking about, you know why you're here," I snapped back. Clearly, he was done with his innocent mage-in-training act.

Helio pouted. "And here I thought it was because you liked me."

I rapped my fingers on the desk and stared into Helio's eyes, fighting the urge to look lower. It wasn't long before he began to shift awkwardly beneath my gaze.

"Minoma." He finally relented, tracing it on the map. "The next piece of the map is in Minoma. In the library, to be exact."

"And you hadn't headed straight there because?"

"You happened to arrive in town as I was about to try to hire a ship." He shrugged. "When you mentioned you were heading to the temple, I figured we may be after the same thing—and I turned out to be right."

I removed my feet from the desk and studied the map, my fingers still tapping. "Well, that's frustrating."

"Not in the Minoman's good books?" he joked.

"Osiria's," I corrected, studying the map.

The fastest way to Minoma from where we were was north and then west, through Osirian waters. With my brother's connections to Isidia and our own tensions with the Dark-Elves, it would not be wise to enter their borders. Going south would add unnecessary time to our journey and take us through uncertain waters, given the current human conflicts.

I sighed and sat back in my chair, pinching the bridge of my nose.

"We could always say I'm the Captain," Helio suggested.

I stared over my hand at him. "My ship is one of the most well-known across the land, do you really think you could get away with pretending to be its captain?"

"It was just a suggestion." He shrugged.

"It was a stupid one." I rose from my chair and paced. "North of here, not far if we catch a good wind, there's a Kushyami port. I know a captain who docks there that may be able to help us." I couldn't stop the grin that spread across my face as memories flooded my mind. "They may not be so happy to see us, but I can convince them. They make a lot of deliveries to Osiria. We'll hide in the ship, act as crew, whatever, and get them to sail on to Minoma."

"And once we're in Minoma and have the map piece?" Helio asked, rising from the chair, his eyes bright at the possibility of success.

"We'll hire a crew there to take us the rest of the way and return to Kushyam once we've got the goods."

"And, just so we're clear, would the Captain be unhappy to see you and the crew, or just you?"

"We've got a … complicated past, to put it lightly."

"That bodes well," Helio said, voice laden with sarcasm.

"Don't have another option," I said cheerily, slapping his shoulder, hard enough to make him unsteady on his feet, as I strolled past him. "Jarrell!" I called over the deck from my cabin door.

"Aye, Captain?"

"Set a course for Kushyam. Teresh Port."

"Aye, Captain," Jarrell said apprehensively.

I shot him a stern look, my patience wearing thin. Everyone on my ship had been far too happy to question me lately. He offered a curt nod and began shouting orders at the crew. I turned back to face the Osirian in my cabin. He was standing by the small bookshelf on the starboard side of the room, picking at the spines of my books.

He seemed altogether too comfortable in my space, as if he thought himself untouchable. Despite his lean figure, he was not weak, I knew that now—given how far he'd managed to swim and how quickly he'd recovered. His skin was a redder shade of purple than usual for Dark-Elves, indicating time spent in the sun; the speckling of freckles across his nose and cheeks supported my theory.

"Tell me who you really are." I said, leaning back against my desk, my arms extended back to support my weight.

Helio seemed surprised by my casualness and composure in his presence, no doubt used to the usual fear and defensiveness people tended to direct toward Osirians. "I told you, I'm a scholar."

"Scholars don't tend to climb mountains, pick fights with ship captains, and hunt   for   treasure." He plucked a book off the shelf and flicked through some of the pages. "I'm dedicated," he said, running a finger down a page as if he were reading it.

"And what about your incredible sea legs?" I asked, having noticed the smoothness with which he moved onboard. People who were new to ships, or rarely boarded, could take hours, if not days, to get used to the constant rocking of the vessel, no matter how slight it may be.

"Well, if you must know, I spent a few miserable years in the Osirian navy."

"Ah. A deserter." I crossed my ankles.

Helio slammed the book shut and placed it back on the shelf before him, his eyes clashing with mine when he turned and ran a finger along the spines on the shelf as he walked toward me.

My fingertips tingled at the tonal shift within the room.

"I didn't desert. I was discharged."

I was surprised at the sudden spike of anger in his tone, but it was exactly what I'd wanted. How far could I push him before he'd break? "Couldn't handle the heat?"

Rage sparked in his amber eyes. "Couldn't handle the corruption, the lies, the bullshit." He stopped beside me, placing a hand near mine and leaning toward me. "Everyone treats us like monsters, but that just means they've never fought against Carracallans at sea."

I leaned closer into his face, sharing his breath. "War is war. Your lot aren't so nice to fight against, either, as I'm sure you can imagine."

"Oh, sure, I'm with you on that. Especially when your admiral sends entire fleets out on suicide missions that leave whole crews either Naeinn or dead." His eyes drifted with the words, his mind carried off to past memories of horror.

I shifted my hand to rest against his on the desk, it was shaking, as was my own. My mind, too, ran red with the horrors of war. Corpses drifting in the water, some whole, others blasted into pieces by cannon fire. The sea around the vessels stained red with blood, the air filled with the screams of the Naeinn, elves driven to madness from the overuse of their magic. Having to return home to tell families, friends, and lovers of their losses, tell them that their loved ones died heroes— while knowing most of them died with piss and shit running down their legs, crying for whoever they believed would bring them comfort in their last moments. Helio didn't move his hand away, didn't step back, but stared at me curiously, the anger gone from his eyes.

For a moment, we were no longer two greedy people seeking the same prize and the glory that would come with it, but two soldiers sharing mutual pain. This was the Helio from the temple gardens, potentially the real Helio, but only time would tell.

I was curious enough to wait.

We snapped out of our moment when a hollow growl echoed through the cabin.

I pulled my hand away, rising from the desk, and Helio stepped back. "The galley is below. With your history, I'm sure I don't need to give you a tour of the ship."

"Not at all," he said, still holding my eyes, seemingly searching them for some kind of answer.

"I will warn you, our cook is Isidian, ex-navy—had an extra bad run-in with Osirians."

Helio nodded. "Jarrell is your first mate?"

I nodded.

"I'll seek his assistance."

I nodded once more and, with one last searching look, he left.

At last collapsing onto my bed, I fought against the memories that had resurfaced—and with them the longing for a drink. The shaking of my hands had not only been due to reliving the trauma unexpectedly, but the desire to wrap around the neck of a bottle, the handle of a flagon, the stem of a goblet.

I became, all of a sudden, too aware of the sweat on my skin, the emptiness of my stomach. Nausea hit me like the waves of a storm hit the deck. I needed a distraction, something—anything—to do, but I felt so ill I couldn't move. I slammed my pillow over my face and prayed the sickness would go away.

CHAPTER

II

"Bell."

I groaned and turned over in my bed, facing the wall.

"Bell, I've got water and food," Peverell coaxed. "I can bring tea."

I grunted.

"All right, I'll go and get you tea, and then we need to talk."

I heard him place down the food and water, then leave the room. The second the door clicked shut, I turned back toward the room, shielding my eyes from the afternoon sun, and stuffed as much food in my mouth as possible, the bread settling my stomach almost instantly. But the water pushed it too far.

I rushed to the galley windows, flinging one open, and vomited down the stern of the ship.

"Do you want me to get you some wine?" Peverell asked from behind me.

"No," I said sternly, wiping my mouth and turning from the window. "I'm fine."

"I really think you should have some. Cutting it all out at once can do more harm than good."

"I said I'm fine." I stalked to my desk and waited for him to place the tea down before me. "This isn't my first time, I know what works."

Peverell's fingers tapped on the tray as he stared at me, his mind no doubt running through thousands of things he'd read about sobriety and how to achieve it. "Well, hopefully the tea will help, then," he said and placed the tray down.

I eagerly reached for the pot and filled my cup, sipping the amber liquid and sighing as it dissolved the coating of vomit that lingered in my mouth. "Now, what did you want to talk about? And keep it brief."

"The Osirian," he said flatly. "What are we going to do about him?"

"Why?" I asked. "Wanna kill 'im?" I watched him over my cup as I took a sip.

Peverell looked as if he was considering it for a moment, but gave a light shake of his head before saying, "No, I just don't understand why we're keeping him around if he's told us what we need to know."

"I think he knows more than he's letting on, and I don't want to be left in the lurch."

"So, you trust him?"

I thought on that for a moment. "I wouldn't say trust … I'm curious. I want to see how long he thinks he can get away with hiding things from me."

"Bellona." Peverell groaned, his face in his hands. "An Osirian is not someone you keep around because of curiosity."

I drummed my fingers on the side of the teacup. "Regardless, we may need him."

"I don't trust him."

"I don't care," I bit back. "He stays."

"You two sound as if you're arguing over a pet," Jarrell cut in.

"Am I no longer the Captain of this ship? Since when do you just stroll in here unannounced?"

"Apologies, Captain. I was also curious about the Dark-Elf and knew His Highness had come to speak to you about him."

I saw Peverell flinch slightly at Jarrell's words and decided, for my own peace of mind, to ignore it. "Well, since I am still the Captain of this ship, I say he's staying, you all have to deal with it, and I'll hear no more about it." I slammed my teacup down on the table, the porcelain almost shattering at the force.

"By your orders, Captain," Jarrell said with a nod. "We'll arrive at Teresh in a week's time, wind permitting." Jarrell hovered in the doorway silently for a moment before adding, "All I'll say on the matter is, he knows his way around a ship—"

"He was in the na—" Jarrell silenced me with a raised hand, and I wondered why I felt the need to defend him anyway.

"Beyond what they teach in the navy, Captain," he said and left my cabin.

I thought of the few details Helio had given me of his time in the navy and hoped he hadn't been one of the Admirals to send fleets of ships to their doom.

"We just want you to be careful," Peverell said.

"I am careful," I ground out, just as my stomach turned. I gagged and choked on the vomit that rose unexpectedly, coughing it onto the table between my brother and me.

"Bellona?!" Peverell cried, pushing away from the desk and coming to stand behind me.

Pain lanced through my middle. I curled up and fell to the side, off my chair. Peverell caught my head just moments before it would've hit the ground.

There was a bang and rushing footsteps.

"She's been poisoned!" Helio exclaimed, rushing to my side.

"How?" Peverell demanded suspiciously.

Helio pushed my brother out of the way and knelt beside me on the floor, he began patting my body, running his hands over my back and arms.

"Get your hands off my sister!" Peverell raged, about to swing a fist at Helio's head when I gasped in pain as Helio touched the wound on my shoulder. Peverell lowered his arm, staring in disbelief as the Osirian ripped my shirt and began to heal me. "How did you know?" Peverell asked.

"The dart from the deck." Helio grunted as he focused his energy on healing me, the dark mass of his magic lining my peripherals. "I picked it up as I climbed aboard, I thought it had just been a warning shot, like the others, but I studied the end and found it to be coated in some kind of salve."

"I hadn't even known she'd been hit."

I gasped as the pain again arced through my stomach, and Helio grunted, then cursed. "Get the Isidian, I'm not strong enough to heal this."

Peverell rose and darted from the room, his boots hitting the floor by my head. The noise sent searing pain through my skull and I whimpered.

"It's all right, Bellona," Helio soothed.

I tried to lift my head to look at him but couldn't, my whole body felt weighed down by some invisible force. I clawed at the floorboards, as if breaking through them would free me of the pain scoring its way through my body. The door banged open again, and more loud footsteps followed, I cried out in pain as the noise struck me once more.

"Watch out, Deathbringer," Halen said as he hobbled behind me, grunting as he lowered himself to the floor to reach my shoulder, light flaring through my closed eyelids as he took over the healing of my wound. His magic coursed through my body, reaching further than Helio's had, and finally dulled the pain. "Why didn't you tell us sooner?" Halen snapped at Helio.

"It took me a while to study the dart and then assess which poison had been used—I came as soon as I knew, but it had already taken effect."

"I could have helped," Peverell added. "Why didn't you seek me out?"

"Time sensitivity. I wasn't sure which brother you were, and didn't want to waste the time had you been either of the others," Helio said bluntly.

"And your findings?" Peverell pushed.

"Wolfsbane, or something similar—a human would have been dead hours ago."

"She will be fine then," Peverell said, his tone calming. "But she will need rest, even after the healing the poison will need to work its own way out of her system."

"Surely, it already has," I croaked, my throat raw from vomiting.

"Unfortunately not," Peverell said gently as he pushed my sweat-wet hair from my face. "It could take days. You *will* rest," he said forcefully.

"The ship—"

"Jarrell and Riston will run the ship in your stead. It's what they're here for, after all."

"And I will work with Prince Peverell on his translations and make a plan for Minoma," Helio said.

Peverell glanced at him, suspicion and confusion written across his face.

"Right, I've done what I can. The poison's most of the way through her system already. If you have any more pain, Captain, just call for me and I can dull it," Halen said, giving my healed shoulder a pat.

"Thank you, Halen," I said, moving to rise, but before I could even move my arms to lift myself I was swept from the ground by a pair of purple ones.

Helio carried me to my bed and laid me down gently. I glanced past him and saw Peverell's shocked expression matching my own. Helio pulled my blanket up around me and further pushed my hair back from my face.

"I'll keep watch over her and call if anything happens," he said, not facing my brother or Halen as he said it.

I watched Peverell. Halen laid a hand on his shoulder as he walked past him to leave the room, and my brother just stood, dumbfounded for a moment. I met his eyes and gave a slight nod, indicating that it was fine, that I would be all right. He cleared his throat and left the room.

Helio moved the armchair from under the windows to sit beside my bed. I studied him. I was significantly bigger than him in size and yet, he'd lifted me as if I weighed nothing.

"You don't have to stay with me," I said, my voice shaking. "I really am fine."

He glanced down at me, his golden eyes betraying his carefully emotionless expression. "I should have said something earlier."

"You couldn't have known it was poisoned," I said, jaw chattering, and tucked my shaking hands beneath the blanket, trying desperately to conserve any warmth I could get. Coldness had spread over me without warning, my body shaking violently in response.

"Are you all right?" Helio asked, reaching forward to feel the temperature of my forehead with the backside of his hand. "You're freezing."

I moved over in the bed, regretting it the second my body left the small warm patch I'd made. "Get in."

"What?"

"G-get in the f-fuck-king bed." I struggled to get the words out of my chattering mouth. "I n-need your w-warmth."

"Fine," he said, removing his boots and joining me in the bed, shifting as close to my form as he could without touching me. "You stink like vomit."

"Shut up," I said and wrapped myself around his stiff form. My shaking instantly calmed. Helio was as warm as if he'd just come from standing in the sun or before a hearth. I sighed, my head resting heavily on his shoulder.

"Oh gods, your breath is awful," he whined, but his arm came around me and rested on my shoulder blade as my eyes flitted shut.

CHAPTER 12

The ship lurched, flinging me bodily off the bed and tossing unsecured books and scrolls off my desk. I groaned in pain on the floor as I came to my senses. My whole body still ached from the poison and the exertion of vomiting.

I was cold again and alone.

The ship was swaying dangerously in the turbulent sea, wind and rain lashing the sides. I hoped my crew was safe, but wished I could have been out there to sail us through the storm. Even tied, the wind could be destroying our sails. It would have been better to use them till they couldn't be used anymore—now more time would be wasted repairing them.

The Siren rocked to the side again, creaking with the force of the waves. I wasn't strong enough to fight it and rolled until my side hit the leg of my desk, leaving me gasping.

"Bellona!"

"Peverell …" I groaned, weakly reaching for him. The wind and rain was so loud I hadn't heard the door bang open, nor slam shut, but felt the burst of wind and a few droplets of rain on the backs of my feet.

Arms lifted me and soon I was seated on the bed, resting against my brother's side, his arm wrapped securely around me.

"You're cold as ice," he said, rubbing a hand up and down my arm to generate warmth. "I didn't think I'd be needed so urgently. I'd have come sooner, otherwise."

"Where's Helio?" I asked, my voice a mere shaking whisper.

"That madman," Peverell scoffed. "Attempting to sail the ship through this storm. I wager we won't have to worry about him anymore come morning."

I wanted to be outraged that someone I barely knew was handling my ship, but I wasn't. It would take an extremely skilled sailor to navigate this storm. If he survived, it would be more proof that he had further lied to me, and if he was lost … well, he'd be no concern anymore. I only wished he was still with me. Peverell was as warm as a fish in a barrel, and though it was enough to help, I craved the warmth that had come from Helio.

"Blanket," I pleaded, and Peverell pulled one up and wrapped it about my shoulders before wrapping his arm even more tightly around me as the ship once again lurched to the side. "He better not fucking capsize us," I bit out.

Morning came and I woke to the sun brightly filling my cabin, and warmth beneath the right side of my face and chest. I made to stretch but pulled my legs back up as they touched something at the end of my bed. I lifted my head and looked down. Peverell was curled at my feet, his back to me, breathing softly. Across from me, in the armchair, Helio sat asleep, his arm rested on the bed. In my sleep, I must have reached for its warmth—my face rested on his forearm, his limp hand pulled against my chest by my own. Before I could push it away and feign ignorance, there was a chuckle.

"Morning, Princess," Helio said quietly, careful not to wake Peverell. The morning sun glinted brightly off his white hair, so much so it was almost hard to look at him.

"You're still alive," I said as plainly as possible, leaving it to him to discern the meaning of my words.

His other hand came down to tuck stray hairs behind my ear. "Were you worried?" he asked with a grin. In the morning light, his freckles stood out starkly against his purple skin.

"For the sake of my ship, yes." I deflected, hoping my cheeks were bright enough with fever to hide my blush.

"Your ship is fine, as is your crew. I sent them below before I took the helm. The sails didn't get too destroyed, they may have already been repaired by now."

"I suppose I should thank you."

Helio held up a hand. "Consider it payback for your poisoning."

"Fine. I hate saying it anyway," I said, finally releasing his hand and rolling onto my back. Not that he'd seemed to mind my holding it—I'd forgotten I was.

"How are you feeling?" he asked.

"All right." I paused to assess. "My head's a little sore, I feel like I could throw up, and I think my side is bruised but, other than all that, well enough."

"Your side?"

"Hit it in the storm," I said dismissively. "I'll have Halen heal it."

"I'll go and fetch him," he said, rising stiffly from the armchair. "Wish me luck." He winked and strolled off to fetch the Isidian.

As the door closed, Peverell's head snapped up and he turned to face me. "Bellona," he said, "I don't like how friendly you're getting with him."

I rolled my eyes and pushed Peverell off the end of my bed, grunting when he landed on the floor with a thud.

"He can't be trusted!" He continued with barely a reaction, rising from the floor, rubbing his shoulder.

"Because he's Osirian?" I challenged.

Peverell paused for a moment. It was something I was grudgingly coming to appreciate about him, his willingness to be questioned without ego. "Because," he continued carefully, "he's clearly after the bracelet." He kept his voice low, glancing toward the door.

I rolled my eyes. Never mind. "I'm not a fucking idiot, of course he's after the bracelet," I said, pulling myself up to sit against the wall of my cabin. "He could have killed me last night, easily, and blamed it on the poison, but he didn't."

"That does not mean he's harmless."

"No. But it means he knows more than he's revealed and he needs me."

Peverell stared at me dubiously.

"Why else would he keep me alive? He's had multiple opportunities to kill me. Bring me my pipe, would you?"

He sighed, but walked over to my desk and fished in the draws for everything I needed.

"I can't say I've been a difficult target, but he's kept me alive, purposefully," I said as I packed the bowl of my pipe. "There must be something my gills are needed for." I took a long draw, the smoke tingling my throat as I sucked it down. "I'm in no danger from him, and I don't need you looking out for me," I said, smoke curling about my mouth as I spoke. "Question me again and you'll end up in the brig."

"Your threats are growing empty, Bellona."

"I assure you they are not, brother." I placed the bit in my mouth, drawing deeply again as Halen came through the door.

Peverell gave me one last challenging look before leaving, shouldering Helio on the way out. I watched as Jarrell met him on the deck and followed him below. I pinched the bridge of my nose and sighed deeply.

"Captain, I've been told you need more healing," Halen said as he reached the side of the bed. I simply nodded and lifted my shirt to show the bruised side, my pipe dangling from my mouth. "I would have advised against smoking while the poison was still present," he chided.

"You wouldn't like me if I didn't," I said with a grin.

Halen healed my side and checked the poison levels, reporting that there were still remnants and I should remain in bed for the rest of the day, but he was surprised at how well my body had recovered overnight. He left, promising food and tea, and closed the door behind him, ignoring Helio's existence entirely.

"Charming fellow," Helio said, once again sitting in the armchair beside the bed.

"I did warn you," I murmured around my pipe bit as I smoothed my hands through my hair, pushing it away from my face. Helio's eyes lingered on the pipe, and when my hands were free, I took it from my mouth and offered it to him. He took a deep draw.

As the smoke filled his chest, I saw concern spread across his face and laughed as he broke into fits of coughing. "A special Carracallan blend," I informed him, "not for the weak."

"Clearly," he rasped, handing the pipe back. "The Osirian leaf is much smoother."

"Can't say I've had the pleasure," I said, drawing more smoke into my chest, the pain in my head subsiding slightly, "but I'm open to new things." I exhaled, releasing the smoke. It curled between us, reaching out as if to caress Helio.

"Good to know," he said, sitting back in the armchair and closing his eyes, his hands gripping the armrests, knuckles white.

I grinned to myself as I smoked the rest of the leaf in the bowl.

CHAPTER

13

Moonlight shone through the gallery windows of the great cabin. Peverell, Jarrell, Helio, and I sat around a map spread across the end of the large table. Unlike other ships of the same build, *The Siren* was plain in its decor. I was a practical person and saw little point in decorating a room that was only to be used by me and my crew, and my brothers had known this when they'd ordered her to be built.

"So, the plan," I said, clapping my hands together and leaning back in my chair. "Helio, Peverell, Zandra, and I will disembark in Kushyam and seek out Captain Ikram. We'll convince them to sail us through Osirian waters to Minoma, where we will retrieve the last piece of the map. Peverell and Helio can translate it, then we'll hire a ship and crew and meet back here."

"Why Zandra?" Jarrell asked.

"We can use her as a reason for needing to go to Minoma."

Peverell looked slightly horrified, but was silent as he thought it all through. I was happy with the plan Helio and I had concocted, but part of me had hoped that Pev would come up with something that kept him safely on board *The Siren*.

"I don't see any issues with that," he said at length.

My eyebrows rose. "You sure about that? 'Cause if you've got a better idea, we'd be open to hearing it."

"No-no, I think it's a good plan."

"With all due respect, Your Highness," Jarrell cut in, "I don't. Captain, the Prince is not as capable as you, not as … worldly. I think it best he stay here." There was clearly more he wanted to say, but stopped himself, his gaze flicking quickly to my brother and back to me.

"Excuse me, sir, I am every bit as capable as my sister. Not having spent a whole life at sea does not diminish the time I have spent. I survived my first voyage, same as you."

"Oh sure, but if shit goes south can you handle a sword?" Jarrell countered.

I was about to rise to my brother's defense, to scold my first mate for addressing his prince in such a manner when Peverell threw his chair back.

"Would you like to see how well I can handle a sword?" he said, his anger clear on his face. "You think I only enjoy studies of dead languages and poetry? I'm probably the best swordsman on this ship."

"I'm not going to duel you, Peverell," Jarrell said flatly.

"I'm going with you, Bellona, whether your first mate thinks it's a good idea or not," Peverell said, before leaving the room and slamming the door.

"I don't want, or need, to know what's going on between you and my brother, but after that, you need to apologize."

"Captain—"

"He is your prince, regardless of who you are to each other." Jarrell fell silent at my words. "Now, I will need you and the crew to stay in Teresh and we'll meet you back there. Understand?"

"Yes, Captain."

"Good. Now, I want you to relay that order to Riston and tell Zandra of the plan. Make sure she knows to be ready once we make port."

"Yes, Captain. I didn't get to say it before, but I'm also not comfortable with you relying on Captain Ikram, given how things ended with them last time."

"I'll handle Ikram." I waved a hand dismissively.

Jarrell nodded. "I'll make everyone aware of the plan, as discussed," he said and left the room.

I let my head fall and rest on the tabletop.

"Are you feeling all right?" Helio asked.

"Just tired, sick of my brother's bullshit, and I'd do about anything for a drink."

"I didn't think you drank,"

"No. I … I don't drink anymore."

"Ah," he said knowingly.

"But right now, Mother and Father, I could drink a whole town dry." I dug my hands into my scalp and massaged my head. This adventure was meant to be just that, an adventure, but it had turned into one giant excruciating headache. I'd known going into it that Peverell and I would be at each other's throats, but I had expected less fight from him. At least had it been Eevan, I would have known what to expect. Now, the quest itself was adding to the headache.

"Not drinking must be recent if it's causing this big of an issue," Helio commented.

"Very recent, but the poison is also not helping."

"Can I ask why?"

"My sister-in-law told me she would bar me from seeing my niece."

We both seemed surprised at the confession, but I hadn't even considered not telling him. I couldn't pin what it was, but there was just something about Helio that made him so easy to talk to.

"I see." The room went quiet for a moment, save the tapping of Helio's heel, before he continued. "My grandfather was a drinker. Never thought much of it until I was grown and viewed my memories with an adult's gaze. He'd been in the navy as well, though before it had that name … saw terrible things … he never wanted me to join, but I thought it would make him proud."

"Was he a violent drunk?"

"No, just a useless one. My grandmother did everything for us, worked herself into the grave. He followed not long after."

"I s'pose you've stayed off the bottle, then."

"Oh, mostly." He grinned. "I've never really been one to learn from experience, but I try to keep my distance. It runs in the blood you know, the disease. But you can avoid it if you know how to channel it."

"And you've channeled it into your studies?"

"Something like that."

"Perhaps I need to channel it into something else," I said, my eyes raking down Helio's lean figure, searching for hints of the muscles hidden beneath his clothes.

"A craft of sorts," Helio teased, leaning back in his chair and lifting his hands to rest behind his head. The edge of his shirt lifted and I wanted, so desperately, to slip my hands under it and run them up his chest.

"Never been one for crafts," I said, leaning into his openness. Had there not been a table between us, I'd have been sitting on his lap already, or he on mine, whichever he preferred.

"Some other activity, then," his gaze met mine and the air between us seemed to hum.

Both our intentions were clear, our gazes dripping with desire, but who would make the first move? We were still for three heartbeats, then his elbow lowered slightly, and that was all it took. Instantly, I was pushing the maps out of the way, making sure not to knock any candles, and climbing across the table. He met me halfway, his haste reflecting my own.

We crashed together in the middle of the table, there was nothing delicate or slow about it, it was hungry and feral. I gripped a fistful of his hair at the root and pulled his face from mine. He gasped, his own hands gripping my hips tightly as I kissed down his neck. He ground his hips against mine, making sure I felt exactly how much he was enjoying what I was doing. I grinned against his clavicle and released his hair, running my hand down until I could fix it around his throat, bringing my lips back to his and squeezing.

He let out a whimper of pleasure and fell back, pulling me over him, his fingers digging into the backs of my thighs. I groaned as I straddled him and felt his hardness against me. We both moaned and gasped with pleasure as we ground against each other atop the table, all the while our tongues battling for dominance during our ravenous kisses.

This was exactly the type of distraction I needed. I moved to remove my pants so we could take it further. Helio reached to assist with one of his hands, the other gripping my wrist at his throat tightly, the message clear—don't let go. I grinned and squeezed, looking down, focusing on our hands working together to unlace my pants when a sharp pain shot through my head. I gasped at the pain, my grip loosening anyway as I swayed.

"Bellona, are you all right?"

"My head—" My hands flew to my head as pain lanced through it again. Helio slid out from beneath me and helped me down from the table, leading me back through the gun deck to the main deck and into my cabin, calling for Halen along the way.

"The poison is almost out of your system," Halen said as the white mist cleared from my vision. "But you still need to take it easy, don't over-exert yourself—especially if you want to be well enough for Kushyam," he warned before leaving.

I sighed and slumped against my pillows. "Why couldn't the poison have been something that didn't affect us?"

"Well, it could be worse. If you were human, you'd have been dead."

"Fair," I said, gazing over at Helio, who was once again scanning my bookshelf. "Looking for anything in particular?"

"You don't have any reading books," he commented.

"I'm not a big reader."

"What do you do when you're out at sea if you don't read and you don't craft?"

"Literally anything else," I said closing my eyes.

"Seems dull."

"Well, usually I'm not poisoned and can swim. I like swimming," I said as the world began to fade away.

I couldn't be sure if it was real Helio or dream Helio, but one of them said, "Good to know," in a quiet voice.

CHAPTER
14

Teresh Port cut across the horizon, the morning sun shining across the docks and glinting off the gems and precious metals that were being loaded onto ships. It was a pirate's dream, all this excess out in the open, but the Kushyami guards, with their whips, spears, and khopesh in hand, were enough to deter anyone. They lined the docks from shore to sea, almost daring someone to try and steal.

It was mid-morning by the time we'd fully docked. Jarrell was nowhere to be seen, so I told Riston that Helio and I were heading out to speak with Ikram and we made our way through the docks till we found *The Duat*. It was a smaller vessel than you'd expect, with guns only visible on the main deck. The only windows were at the back of the ship and were located in the captain's cabin. The rest of the ship was a floating safe and cramped living quarters, though due to the heat, the crew mostly slept on the open deck, rather than below.

"Captain Glenon. We didn't know you were in Teresh," one of the ship's crew said as I made my way to their gangplank.

"We only arrived this morning. I was hoping to speak with your Captain."

The Kushyami looked past my shoulder at Helio and then back to me. "I don't know if the Captain will want to speak with you."

"Well, I'm sure you could convince them and lightly remind them that they owe me a debt."

"I will check with them. If you could just wait here a moment," they said before darting up the plank and disappearing on the deck.

"C'mon, Ikram," I muttered to myself.

"Is this going to work, Bellona?" Helio whispered.

"Yes, they owe me. I didn't piss them off enough for them to forget that."

"The Captain will speak with you!" The crew member called down to us.

I waved my acknowledgment and made my way up the gangplank. The crew were darting around the deck, preparing for cast-off, but they were a long way off. Knowing Ikram, they'd leave just before sunset so they could watch the sun sink over the land as they sailed north.

There were no castles on this deck, so the crewman led us below and to the stern of the vessel, knocking on the door and announcing our presence to the Captain before retreating speedily. Helio and I shared a slightly worried look before I shook out my shoulders and entered the room.

"Ikram!" I said by way of greeting, my arms out before me in an open gesture— then ducked as an object made its way toward my face and smashed against the wall behind me.

"What do you think you're doing back here?!" Ikram demanded. "And calling in favors!" They spat at the ground by my feet.

"Calling in debts!" I countered, and took a few breaths to calm myself before continuing. "I'm offering for you to pay back the debt you owe me by taking me and some passengers aboard—"

"Is that all?" Ikram sat on their desk, their arms folded over their chest, face held in a scornful, scrunched expression.

"If you'd let me finish?"

Ikram waved an impatient hand.

"We seek passage to Minoma—"

"I don't go to Minoma."

"Let. Me. Finish." I ground out, only continuing once their mouth was firmly shut. "I want to travel through Osirian waters and, given my family's ties to Isidia, I can't do it on my ship."

"And how do you propose we get through the checkpoints? They all know I only go between here and there."

"I have a Minoman on my crew. We'll say she's someone important and has paid for discreet but safe passage home—there's nowhere safer than *The Duat*."

Ikram pushed off the desk and walked around it, gazing at the papers and maps spread across it, working out if this detour would affect the flow of their business.

The cabin was exactly as I remembered it, cluttered and full of obscenely extravagant decor. Gold and gems coated almost every surface, as well as rich rugs and expensive Sillessian fabrics. Ikram themself was dressed in Sillessian garb, rather than Kushyami. Their purple top and pants were embroidered with silver thread that glittered when they moved through the streams of light coming through the windows, though they'd forgone the pleated wrap that was usually worn with the ensemble.

"I suppose," they finally said, "it wouldn't leave us too far off course. We could catch up." They fiddled with one of the many necklaces they wore. "Though I don't know if I would consider my debt worth the whole journey … What else can I get from this?"

"My respect and gratitude?" I offered.

"As if that's worth anything," they murmured.

"Fine. What do you want, Ikram?"

"No lies, no secrets. I want to know why you need to go to Minoma. Tell me that and we're fine—unless it's really dangerous and could fuck me over."

I chewed on the inside of my cheek. We needed them to help us, but I wasn't ready to deal with another interested party.

"We're looking for the last piece of an ancient treasure map," Helio said.

Ikram looked at him as if they'd only just noticed his presence and then laughed, loud and booming, "A treasure map? Bellona, you've got to be kidding me?"

"What can I say?" I said, shooting a cold look at Helio over my shoulder.

"Well, if it's for something as stupid as that, I'll take you on, but you have to stay below deck and out of sight at the checkpoints. The guards know me and my crew, they trust us, they'll barely bother to check."

"Thank you, Ikram." I bowed. "I'll collect the others and be back here just past noon."

The Captain nodded and waved us out of their cabin. I turned, grabbed Helio by the shoulders and steered him off the ship.

"What the fuck were you thinking? What if they decided they wanted a share of the treasure?" I whispered as we stalked back to *The Siren*.

"I knew they'd think it was bullshit, and what would they care? Did you see all the shit in that room? They don't care about having to hunt for treasure."

It was a fair assessment, but a risk even I would not have taken. "Next time, just let me do the talking," I shot back, speeding up till he was practically jogging to keep up.

"Cerys!" I called once we were on the ship.

"Captain?"

"Your sister ready to go?"

"Almost, Captain!"

"Very good," I said, making my way across the deck to my cabin, Helio's footsteps close behind me.

"Are you sure you're well enough for this?" he asked, closing the door firmly before facing me.

"I am," I said sternly.

He'd been questioning my health since the night in the great cabin, refusing to go any further than kissing until Halen said I was completely free of the poison. "I just don't want you to get hurt, again," he said, tucking a stray hair behind my ear.

"And I don't want you to fuss over me—I have my brother here for that."

"Where is he? I think I've seen him once since that argument with Jarrell."

"He's probably holed himself up somewhere in the hold to sulk," I said, shoving some spare clothes into a pack. "I'll go and look for him soon." I dumped the pack onto my bed and pulled a box from underneath it. Inside were all my weapons and spare belts. I strapped on a few extra belts and added an array of weapons, daggers, two swords, throwing knives, anything I might need in case of an emergency. I switched out my captain's coat for a leather vest and thin jacket. The coat would not do me well sailing through Kushyami, Osirian, and Minoman waters, even in Shinchaku it had been too thick. I tried to think of what else I could need, but my mind drew blank.

"I'm going to find Peverell. You stay here," I told Helio before kicking the storage box back under my bed and leaving the room.

I scoured the lower decks, but Peverell was nowhere to be found, though evidence of him was everywhere. Ink stains all over the floors in the great cabin, books, and parchment stacked by the galley and the folded hammocks. I stalked to the forecastle, not bothering to knock before barging into my first mate and Bo'san's shared room, but I certainly wished I had.

As the door swung open, I was met with a straight-shot view of my first mate and my brother passionately fucking.

"Mother in her fucking pit!" I exclaimed before shielding my eyes.

"Bellona!"

"Captain, fuck."

"Apologies, gentlemen! Carry on." I said, slamming the door and spinning back to my cabin, my stomach roiling more than it had when I'd been poisoned. I suddenly felt pity for my brothers and all the times they'd walked in on me in such positions—it was awkward enough being the one caught, but to be the one doing the catching?

Helio was sitting in the chair at my desk, his feet raised, and a book set upon his knees. He glanced over the top of it at me and laughed.

"They were fucking, weren't they?" He laughed only harder at my confirmation. "I wondered how long it would take them. They've been panting after each other for weeks."

I groaned. "Please, do not speak of it."

"I bet you want a drink now!" He laughed, closing the book and taking his feet from the desk. "I could get one for you," he said, stepping toward me, "or I could distract you."

"That is the very last thing on my mind right now. In fact, I'm thinking I may become a priest."

"Was it that bad?"

"I guess you don't have any siblings."

"No, I don't, and by the look on your face, I should be glad that I don't."

"So, so glad." I sat on my bed, scrubbing my eyes, hoping to etch away the image of what I'd just witnessed.

"To think, they've only just consummated their relationship and now they're to be separated for Mother knows how long," Helio mused wistfully. "How tragic."

I made a gagging noise and shoved my pillow over my face, hoping it would drown out the sound of his laughter and what I thought was a bed scraping against the deck.

CHAPTER
15

Ikram had given us access to two cabins below deck—after I complained about having to share one with my brother—and directed that we were not to leave them when going through a checkpoint, but at all other times we were free to roam the upper deck. The rooms were small but quiet and, more importantly, secure, having been originally built as extra safe rooms for the precious cargo handled by the ship. There was enough room in each to hang two hammocks and set up a small table and chair. We had originally planned to have Zandra and I share, but she and Helio switched after he complained of my brother continually glaring at him.

"I swear you two are children," I murmured from my hammock.

"I could say the same of you," Helio replied from his seat at the table. Peverell had given him some text to translate from the second piece of the map and, from my position in my hammock, I could see that he was struggling. "Jarrell apologized."

"Apologies can't erase what I saw. It's burned into my memory forever," I sulked.

Helio rolled his eyes and got back to his translating, the sound of his quill scratching across his notepad filling our cabin, my shoulders inching slightly higher each time it clinked against the inkwell before continuing its incessant journey across the page. I swung down from my hammock and left the cabin. We were going to be on this ship for at least a week, if we had good wind, and I was not prepared to spend the whole time locked in a tiny room with that sound.

The crew on deck were busy setting the sails for the night and laying out their rolls and hammocks for sleep. The air on deck was warm, but thankfully not uncomfortably so. I could have happily slept out in the open with the crew, but it was not safe; we could not be sure if and when the Osirian patrols could stumble upon us, even though we were still very much in Kushyami waters. The Osirians were not ones to stick behind their own borders when it came to the ocean.

Ikram waved me over to the quarter deck, where they were watching their crew at work. "Out of hiding?" they asked as I approached.

"I wasn't hiding, I was resting. I told you—I've been ill recently," I said, keeping the fact that I had been poisoned to myself.

"Yes, I do hope you're feeling better," Ikram said, though there was a touch of salt in their tone.

"I really appreciate you doing this for me, Captain. I hope you know how grateful I am."

"Yes, grateful. Well, it's always a pleasure to have you on board. And I'm sure we won't run into the same issue we did last time?"

I resisted the urge to roll my eyes. "Ikram, I can't control where pirates come from."

"No, but you can control whether or not they make it into your bed. Especially when it's not even your bed!"

"I thought they were you!"

"They were half my size, Bellona."

"I was not in a state of mind where I would have noticed that and you know it." I took a deep breath, "I'm sorry, it wasn't your fault. I can barely remember what happened, to be perfectly honest, but I'm sorry."

Ikram considered this for a moment, their brown eyes set on my face. "Well, if we're apologizing, I should probably admit that I overreacted. Leaving you in the middle of the ocean and shooting cannons was a bit dramatic."

"I would agree, though I was the one being shot at," I joked. "We were both terrible to each other, but we've apologized and it can now be put behind us."

Ikram reached out and flicked some dust off my shoulder. "Have dinner in my cabin tonight," they said. It wasn't a question so much as an open invite. "Despite my reaction, I was sad to see you go all those months ago."

"Pardon me if I didn't quite share that sentiment."

Ikram laughed. "No, I suppose you wouldn't have, in the moment, but … surely over time you've missed me?"

"Ikram … perhaps there was a time but …"

They reached out and took my hands in theirs. "Have dinner with me. Just dinner."

"Just dinner," I agreed with a smile.

I nipped back to my cabin to at least brush my hair before dinner. Helio was still diligently working on the translation; from the ink stains that coated his hands and the text that was almost covering the whole page before him, I assumed he was making some headway.

"I was just about to head up to grab some food. Come with me?" he asked, wiping his quill clean with a dirty rag.

"I'm actually having dinner with the Captain." I tucked in my shirt, then leaned over to straighten my boots.

"Oh. I thought you weren't on particularly good terms."

I pretended I couldn't understand the true question behind his words. "We talked it over—though it felt almost too easy." I smirked and slapped my thighs as I stood. "If I don't return tonight, perhaps warn my brother," I said, opening the door, but paused when Helio gripped my hand.

"Bellona," he said gently, his gold eyes meeting mine with an intensity that made me want to look away, "Be careful."

"I always am." I said with a grin, pulling my hand from his and continuing on to the captain's cabin.

The captain's cabin glowed brighter than the Kushyami throne room with all the candles lit, the light glinting off every golden and bejeweled surface, leaving small rainbows and reflections of colored light on the ceilings and walls. The space was so packed full of shit that there was nowhere to set up a proper table, so two places had been set on either side of the desk, with Ikram already seated at one.

"Evening, Captain," I said as I slowly took my seat, eyeing the set-up meaningfully.

"I hope this arrangement is all right, I just wanted some more time to speak, just the two of us."

I raised an eyebrow and sipped from a tankard of water.

"This ... treasure map, is it real or is it some fantasy of the Osirian's?" they asked.

"Why do you care?"

"Well, if there's treasure"—they gestured around the room—"I'm sure you can see why I'm interested. And if it's just the Osirian, well, maybe I'm just curious. As you said, your family is very much associated with Isidians, so you travelling openly with an Osirian is very ... surprising." They gazed at me over their wine goblet, eyes glinting in the candlelight.

I didn't know what to say. I should have known that the second treasure was mentioned, their senses would have pricked. "He's just a stray we picked up along the way," I deflected.

"You're not usually one to pick up strays."

"This one was persistent."

"You do like persistence," Ikram said with a grin. "Now, the treasure—what is it?"

I ran my fingers across the wood grain of the tankard. Ikram would know if I lied—I'd put us in this situation, and there was no skirting around it. I could get off this ship, could swim all the way to Minoma, but my brother, Zandra, and Helio could not. "Well, we can't be sure, but it seems to be something old of goblin origin."

Ikram sat back in their chair, running a finger along the top edge of their goblet. "Goblin treasures tend to either be enchanted ... or cursed. Which are you hoping for?"

I shrugged. "Hadn't thought about it, to be honest. I'm sure you've noticed I don't have my usual brother accompanying me? This was meant to be our last hurrah, but he chose to stay in Isidia."

"So, you leapt into another situation without thinking it through," they stated bluntly. "Will you ever change, Bellona?"

"Would you have me any other way?" I mused, smirking to hide the hurt. Ikram's words were too familiar for my liking.

"If I had a say in the matter," Ikram murmured before having a mouth full of wine.

"You want a stake?" I asked.

"In some dull goblin shit? Mother no."

"Then why take us on?"

"I wanted to see you, make amends, pay my debts. Us humans can't hold on to grudges. We're not here for as long as you elves are, and with the rise in piracy along my route, I'd rather like to have such matters squared away promptly."

We continued with the rest of the dinner quietly. I answered few questions with actual answers and tried my best to keep my tone light, but I was no longer in the mood for company and left when I could. I knew Ikram had hoped I would stay, despite my hinting earlier that I wasn't interested. Part of me felt badly for leaving them, but my mood was so soured that I couldn't seem to pull myself from it.

Helio was startled from his studies when I slammed the door to our shared cabin upon my return, kicking it for good measure. Again, my mind was running in circles, telling me to find a bottle of anything, anything that would distract, take away the shame and pain. Anything that would make me fun again. My whole body was shaking from the longing. I wanted my pipe, but to smoke it I'd have to go above deck and there were too many people; even Helio's presence was irritating.

"Dinner didn't go well?" He asked offhandedly. "I thought you'd be there late."

"What's that supposed to mean?" I shot back.

"Only that you clearly have a past. I saw you holding hands on deck—I assumed further reconciliation was on the table."

"Would it have mattered if it was?"

He dropped his quill and stared at me for a moment, his eyes locking on my face. "No." He said, letting out a breath, his face falling into his hands. "It wouldn't have mattered—shouldn't matter."

"But it does?"

He sighed, raising his head and leaning back in his chair. "I suppose it does." His eyes moved from mine and focused on the ceiling of the cabin. "I shouldn't care, Mother knows I shouldn't, but"—his eyes flicked back to me—"I've never met anyone like you." He laughed. "I'm sure you hear that a lot," he said, rising and crossing the small space to stand before me. "I'm sure I'm not the only one to fall into your snare."

"I didn't realize I was setting one."

"Perhaps that's where the draw comes from." He reached out and ran his hands down my arms.

"Were you jealous?" I asked, as his hands reached mine and I grasped them.

"Immensely," he said as I placed his hands on my hips.

"You didn't need to be," I whispered into his ear, stepping closer to him. His hands moved to grip my arse as I angled his face up to meet mine.

Our lips met and fire filled me.

We were sloppily desperate, crashing against the walls of the cabin in our feeble attempts to touch as much of the other as possible. I forced Helio down onto the table and straddled him, my knees resting on either side of his hips. I ground myself against him and we groaned into each other's mouths, each wanting it as much as the other and not caring if anyone could hear us.

Helio removed my shirt, cupping one of my breasts as he kissed down my neck. I took his hand away and pinned it to the table, catching his mouth with mine again. He smiled against my mouth as I pinned his other hand down and again ground against him, meeting my pressure and moving upward against me as he ran his tongue over my bottom lip, sending a shiver of desire down my spine. Without hesitation, I got down from atop him and removed my pants, instructing him to do the same before resuming our previous position, this time with me sliding down onto him as slowly as I could manage. His eyes rolled back with pleasure, his hands gripping the table beneath him so tightly the purple skin of his knuckles had turned stark white.

Once fully settled, I ran my tongue over his mouth before lightly biting his bottom lip. He released the edge of the table and guided my hand to his throat before returning his own to my arse, lifting me up and then forcing me back down. I grinned at the instruction of what he wanted and obliged, my hand tightening around his neck until his eyes closed with bliss as I rode him at the pace and hardness he'd set.

The thing I loved most about fucking was watching the face of the other party, witnessing their pleasure take over their features as their mind cleared and they lost all ability to think. Helio's face was completely relaxed, his jaw slack and resting against my hand, his brows the least furrowed I'd ever seen them.

It amazed me what power people allowed you to have over them in a moment when they were their most vulnerable. Easily, I could squeeze a little too tight and he would be none the wiser until it was too late. Something about acknowledging the trust he had in me, his eagerness to have my hand so tightly wrapped around his neck, to have his life literally in the palm of my hand, pushed me to a level of ecstasy I'd never experienced before.

I felt myself tighten around him and his mouth fell open in a silent moan as my hips rose faster, lowered harder as I put more pressure on his throat. Helio's fingers dug achingly into my thighs, his nails catching the skin, my body shaking above his as I reached the peak of my pleasure, Helio following soon after. Our cries of gratification were unmuffled, both of us too caught in the moment to even think of suppressing them.

Our bodies were slick with sweat as we took a moment to catch our breaths, my hand moving from Helio's throat now to rest on the table behind him, working to hold myself up—albeit shakily. All I wanted to do was collapse against him, but there wasn't enough room on the table for him to lay back and relax. Helio rose from the table on trembling legs, holding me against him, my legs wrapped tightly around his hips. He dropped the hammocks to the ground and gently lowered us down to them. I was again amazed that he could even lift me, but—now that he was completely naked above me—I was able to see the layer of muscle that had been hidden by his clothes all this time. He wasn't bulky with muscle, like I was, but lean. The kind of strength often easily underestimated.

He kissed me gently as he pulled out and collapsed beside me on the hammock with a sigh. "Fuck."

"Indeed," I returned, still catching my breath.

"Why haven't we been doing that since we met in Shinchaku?"

"Because I was trying to kill you?"

"Oh, yeah. Glad that's in the past," he said, leaning over to kiss my shoulder. It sent a jolt through me.

Despite everything we'd just done, that small, quick peck on the shoulder somehow felt more intimate than anything I'd done with any partner. I glanced over and scanned his face. He was gazing at the ceiling, a look of slight shock had come over his features as if he, too, were stunned by what he'd done. He noticed me watching, forced a smile and took my hand. I smiled back, but let it fall once he'd closed his eyes.

Maybe Peverell had been right, perhaps I was getting closer than I should.

CHAPTER

16

We sailed through the first checkpoint into Osirian waters easily and without question. Once Ikram had done their business at the Osirian ports, however, and it came time to leave Osirian waters and enter Minoman, things didn't go as smoothly as we'd have liked.

The ship had to be anchored so that the Border crews could search it—something we'd been hoping to avoid. Ikram sent a cabin child down to warn us, the poor thing frantically stressing that we were doomed. I had to tell them to smarten up and calm down, that their worry would be our downfall.

"What can we do, Bellona?" Peverell asked, the first words he'd spoken to me since leaving The Siren.

Ikram had said to stay in our rooms if we were boarded, but something told me this was not going to be your average inspection. "We bunker down in the hold, among the ballast. They won't check there," I said.

"How can you be sure?" Peverell stressed.

"I can't, but we don't have another option—unless you want to out yourself and deal with the Deathbringers."

The cabin child flinched and glanced fearfully at Helio.

"They won't go that far, not if Ikram convinces them of Zandra's story," Helio said. "They'll likely check these rooms, though. The hold is our best bet."

"Bring the hammocks," I said. "We can disguise ourselves as a pile of leftovers and just hope they're not in need of some."

Peverell and Helio nodded and set to work collecting our things and taking them down to the hold—we could leave no trace of our presence.

I turned to the child. "Be brave and listen to your captain."

They nodded and took some deep breaths before darting back up to the top deck.

I'd sent Zandra to Ikram days ago so they could work on their tale and relay it to the crew. We could only hope they all did a good job of selling it. I fetched the hammocks and did one last check of the two rooms before joining the others in the hold.

Having been on this ship many times before, it felt odd to venture into the areas usually off-limits, the vaults more often than not filled to the brim with cargo bound either for Osiria or Kushyam. I couldn't help myself and glanced into some of the rooms that came off the main cargo area. Some were regular rooms built up with shelves, but the locks on the doors were heavy; others were lined with iron to form rooms for transporting ice. I was sure to close all the doors inside the vault as I went—the more empty rooms the guards had to check, the quicker they'd get bored and give up. Throwing the hammocks down the ladder first, I climbed down and met Helio and Peverell at the bottom, glad that one of them had thought to bring a lantern.

"We should head toward the bow—even if they check down here, they won't go all the way up there," I said as I retrieved the hammocks and dragged them across the unevenly stacked Ballast stones, Helio and Peverell following closely behind.

The air in the hold was thick and stale, so much so that it was almost difficult to breathe. By the time we reached the bow of the ship, we were all breathing heavily and coated in sweat, but we didn't have time to rest and catch our breath before needing to dive under the hammocks as the sound of shouted orders and booted footsteps thudded along the deck above us.

We laid on our bellies, the hammocks thrown over us, our belongings roughly stacked by our feet, the lantern hurriedly extinguished. I was squished between the two males, their combined body heat only adding to my discomfort, our intermingling breath making the air only thicker and harder to breathe.

The determined footsteps above us moved further down the length of the ship, the sound echoing back to us off the surface of the stacked stones, sometimes accompanied by more muffled barked orders.

We all tensed as we heard the hatch door open at the stern. I glanced at Peverell, barely able to see him in the dark of the hold, but I could see the outline of his head bowed against the rock, could hear the slight movement of his mouth as he prayed.

"This is ridiculous," came a voice from the rear of the ship. "There won't be anything down here, except maybe rats," it moaned.

"Captain said to check everywhere and I'd rather do it than deal with her if we miss something," came the reply.

"To the pit with the Captain," the first voice whined. "No one worth finding would want to be down here."

The second guard laughed. "I'd like to see you say that to her face."

"Fuck it, maybe I will," the first one bit back. "'Captain, this is a waste of time, to the pit with you!' That's what I'll say."

"And the second you finish the last word, you'll be dead and we'll be dropping your bones into the sea."

"Yeah, well, at least I'll have had the last word." They sighed. "I thought Captain Druloks was bad—he was nothing compared to Weth."

At the name, Helio tensed and reached for my hand. I wanted to ask him what was wrong, but the voices of the guards had grown too close, their boots shifting on the stones, the light from their lanterns bleeding through the patched holes in the hammocks. I glanced at Helio. His features were mostly hidden in the dark, but I could see the distant fear sparking in his gold eyes. He was lost, somewhere in the past. The hand that held mine shook, but he managed to keep his breathing quiet—if he was allowing himself to breathe at all.

"Do you feel that?" the second guard asked.

"What?"

"A presence."

The first guard scoffed. "There's hundreds of fucking humans on this ship, of course you feel a presence."

"No, no, down here. It's close."

The Osirians called on their power, and I cursed my stupidity as the light from their lantern darkened. I closed my eyes. I didn't want to see it again, but the memories came flooding back unbidden.

Fleets of ships emerging from clouds of black mist. Hundreds of Carracallan soldiers falling to their knees, choking and gagging as the same black mist was pulled from them and dragged across the sea to merge with the cloud. Black eyes of Osirian soldiers lost to their magic. The screams of the Osirian Naeinn, left to suffer until their commanders finally relented and took them wherever they kept their Naeinn if they even let them live. The hopelessness came crashing down on me, and I could no longer tell if it was Helio's hand or mine that was shaking.

"It's probably just fucking rats. Let's get out of here." The first guard turned and made their way back to the ladder, but the second stepped closer until I heard their footfall right by my head. Their breathing was hard and I worked to keep my own shallow and quiet. I heard the glass panes in the lantern tap against the metal frame as he moved it, searching for whatever life his death magic was sensing. I squeezed Helio's hand, though even touching him made me nauseous after the memories that had replayed in my head only moments before.

"You coming or what?" the first voice called from the stern.

The second guard sighed. "Yeah, yeah, but you're taking the blame if we've missed something."

All three of us relaxed as the sound of boots scraping against rock and then retreating filled our ears. We remained where we were until we heard the footsteps go past above our heads and then fade out of earshot before letting out a collective breath and emerging from beneath the hammocks, gasping gratefully at the—only slightly—fresher air. I pulled my hand from Helio's and shifted away from him, needing some time to collect myself. Peverell came to my side, noticing my distress, and took my hand, using his other to rub my back comfortingly.

Ships and faces still flicked before my eyes, cannon fire sounding in my ears, deafeningly loud. I only knew it was all in my head because the others did not react. I ran a shaking hand over my face, pinching the bridge of my nose as I tried to pull myself from the past, tell myself that the pounding I heard was not soldiers on a deck but my heart.

"Breathe, Bellona," Peverell instructed, the hand holding mine tightening its grip.

I took a deep shuddering breath and blew it out slowly, repeating the process until I felt soothed. "Who is Weth?" I asked Helio eventually, holding my voice firm.

He flinched at the name and focused his eyes on the stones beneath us. "She was my Admiral in the navy," he said and, by his tone, I knew we would not hear more about it.

I gave Peverell a pat on the knee, a small thanks for his comfort, before rising and making my way back to the ladder. "I'll check if it's clear."

Neither argued with me.

I turned once I reached the ladder. Peverell had re-lit the lantern and I could see him gathering our possessions up into a hammock so he could carry them all at once, glancing anxiously over at a solemn Helio. I knew that, despite his distrust of the Dark-Elf, Peverell was fighting the urge to comfort him, to check in and do what he could to help the bad memories pass quicker, as he'd done for me when I'd first returned from war.

The Osirians had left every door open throughout the ship and strewn anything loose about. It made me realize even more how lucky we'd been that my plan had worked. They'd checked everything—even cupboards too small for humans to hide in were flung open, their contents spread across the floor. After what Ikram had said at dinner, I could only assume that they were hunting for proof of piracy. I'd had run-ins with pirates every now and then, but not enough to notice an increase in activity; perhaps it was just that the northern waters were infested. I was about to climb the last set of stairs to the upper deck when the cabin child came crashing down into me, all knees and elbows.

"Woah! Where are you going in such a hurry?" I said quietly, just in case they were being sent to warn me to stay below.

"Captain! I'm sorry. I was rushing to find you. I-I was brave like you told me to be"—they grinned—"and they suspected nothing! They're gone now, but the Captain asks you to stay below deck until they're out of sight."

"Well done," I praised, ruffling their twisted hair. "How did the Minoman woman go?"

"Well enough, from what I saw. I can send her to you if you'd like."

"Yes, please fetch her, and be sure to thank the Captain for me."

They nodded and bounded back up the stairs. Not long after, Zandra came down them, dressed head to toe in Minoman finery.

She dropped onto the stairs before me, her legs spread wide, elbows resting on her knees, her dress falling between her legs. "The sooner I get out of this thing, the better," she whined.

"You look gorgeous." I teased, but she did. Ikram had tied her hair back in a style that consisted of intricate braid work and utilized Zandra's own natural curls to frame her face, her blue eyes contrasting with her tanned skin and dark hair. The sea green dress only further brought out the color of her eyes and the curvaceous shape of her body, resting on one shoulder and cinching at the waist with a jeweled tie that matched a similar one she wore across her brow. "Did they buy it?"

"Buy that I'm gorgeous? Or that I'm some rich idiot sneaking home after a sordid affair with a Kushyami miner?" she asked.

I only raised an eyebrow.

"Well," she continued, "we're still alive, aren't we?"

"That's true," I said, sinking to the floor by her feet and sighing.

"Are you alright, Captain?"

"I'm well enough," I said, resting my head on the wall behind me. "Eager to be off this ship, is all."

It was a partial truth, I did want to be off the ship, but the real issue was having to face old fears. I thought I had worked through my lingering war trauma, but evidently, it was still there, lurking in the depths of my mind. Perhaps it would never leave—or maybe I would wake one day and it would simply be gone.

CHAPTER

17

Minoma was as hot and humid as Shinchaku had been, the grape fields bright with flourishing green vines that spread across the expanse of the horizon and filled the air with a sweet scent. I stood against the railing on the main deck, eyeing the library tower as we sailed past it, tall and white in a sea of terracotta. It was covered in windows, each with a small ledge. It could be climbed if need be, or scaled down in an escape. A window lock was easy enough to pick open; my only concern was dealing with the mages.

Taking one last, deep breath of fresh salty air, I pushed off the railing and headed down to the lower decks. Peverell, Zandra, and Helio were waiting in the empty vault, having set up a table and chairs for the purpose of our meeting. Peverell and Helio sat close with their heads together, discussing the latest revelations from their translating. Zandra sat across from them, leaning back on the rear legs of her chair, whittling a piece of wood with a small knife.

"All right, getting into the library," I said by way of announcing my presence, "how do we do it?"

"Well, Helio is studying there, isn't he? Can't he get us in?" Peverell said, motioning to Helio with his head.

"Helio?"

"I could get us in but … I would risk losing my position at the college. As dedicated as I am to this quest, that is one thing I cannot risk." He seemed somewhat disappointed at the statement, but I couldn't tell if it was because he couldn't help us or because his reputation was on the line.

"We'll just have to break in then," I said matter-of-factly. "Who wants to come with me?" I gazed at each of them. Zandra shrugged and didn't seem interested at all, though her carpentry skills could come in handy. Helio's eyes practically begged to be able to come, even though he'd already said he couldn't, and Peverell seemed to have ignored the question altogether—as if he knew he would not be my first choice so he wasn't going to even bother fighting me on it. I watched as his hand ran over the top of his notebook, over a page of sketches of what he thought the artifact could look like. The final piece of the map could confirm which design was a true representation …

"Peverell, you will come with me."

Zandra raised an eyebrow and glanced at my brother's gobsmacked face.

"What?" Was all he said.

"You'll come with me. Zandra will create a distraction if things go awry, and Helio will find a ship with a crew to carry us the rest of the way. It'll have to be one that's happy to be hired without knowing the heading prior to cast-off and they must be prepared to leave on a moment's notice—we won't be able to stick around."

"Bellona, are you sure?" Peverell asked. "You want me to go with you?"

"Do you not want to?"

He paused for a moment. "I do."

"Good." I looked at the other two. "Happy with the plan?"

"I may already have a ship and crew in mind. They're quite notorious for being unpredictable, but that could play to our advantage," Helio said.

"I can call in a favor with my old mistress—create quite the distraction we will," Zandra said with a sly grin.

"Perfect. You two"—I motioned between Helio and Zandra—"pack our rooms and wait on deck." They nodded and left. "Now, brother, breaking into the library … any ideas?"

Peverell leaned back in his chair and closed his eyes, as if the image of the building was printed on the backs of his lids. Our father did this when he thought deeply; it brought out the features Peverell had inherited from him. It made me think of Eevan, who out of all my brothers most resembled our father. I found I couldn't watch him anymore and looked down at my hands, instead.

"The building is covered in windows, it should be easy enough to break into," Peverell said at length. "Humans have never quite mastered wards, so we won't have to contend with those." He paused for a moment, no doubt sorting through the centuries worth of knowledge stored away in his studious mind. "There are ways we can hide ourselves from the mages so that they can't detect us, but I don't know if we'll be able to access everything we'd need."

"We should be able to get everything in town. If we can't find something, we can give a list to Zandra—she's got connections all over the city."

"How did she end up in your employ?" he asked, sitting forward and opening his eyes.

"She helped me after a hard night. I sought her out the next night to thank her and learned that she and Cerys were struggling, could barely afford rent on Zandra's money and Cerys was struggling to find solid work. So, I took them on. It was just my luck that they were trained carpenters."

"I've never known someone to be as lucky as you, Bell."

I huffed. "Believe me, luck comes at a cost, oftentimes I'd rather be unlucky than have to deal with the consequences."

"Do you think we'll have to scale the tower?"

"Would you be able to if we did?"

"Yes," he said defiantly. "I'm not as physically useless as everyone likes to think I am." His tone was so like Eevan's in that moment, I had to pause and remind myself which brother was in the room with me. I swallowed a stab of guilt, the feeling of betrayal I felt toward Eevan; it wasn't his fault that I had such a dismal relationship with Pev—it was mine. I shouldn't feel as if I were betraying one brother by spending time with another.

Yet, somehow, it felt like I deserved the guilt.

"All right. Let's get ready to go then." Was all I said.

We secured a room in an inn that had a perfect view of the library, where Peverell and I sat at the window staring at the looming tower. Helio had gone straight to find his ship and crew as we'd disembarked *The Duat*, telling us to meet him at the docks when we were ready to leave, and Zandra had left to speak with her ex-mistress. Pipe smoke curled around me, caught on the summer breeze. At first, I had thought simply smashing a window would be enough to get in, but the way the windows were framed would make that too difficult and loud. The library was open to the public, but making our presence known was also a bad idea in my mind.

"Is there a basement at all?" I asked Peverell.

"Not to my knowledge—but surely that would be even harder to access from the outside?"

"Probably. It was just a thought," I murmured around my pipe.

"I honestly think it's as simple as picking a lock and sneaking around."

"If that's what you're happy with," I shrugged, hiding my smile behind the hand gripping my pipe at how much easier this was probably going to be than anything I'd done with Eevan, purely because Peverell actually thought things through.

"Well, if Zandra can bring back those ingredients, it'll be easier still."

"What are they for?" I asked.

Before Zandra had left, Peverell had given her a list of various ingredients and was very insistent on what condition each one needed to be in.

"Well, I should be able to make two things with them, if we can get all the ingredients. A potion that could render us unable to be seen, and one that should make us move without noise."

I choked on my pipe smoke. "What?" I croaked, almost rethinking my earlier sentiments.

"It's human magic. It was deemed too powerful and all knowledge of it was wiped out some millennia ago."

"But, of course, somehow you know about it."

"I know about many things I shouldn't, it's both a gift and a curse."

I shake my head with a snort. "And where exactly did you learn about this?"

"Goblin texts from many thousands of years ago, written in a dialect I suspect only I can read. I found them in the Isidian library but, given the thick coating of dust I had to practically scrape off, I doubt they even knew it was there."

I tapped my fingers on the bowl of my pipe, genuinely impressed despite myself, wondering how the Mother we could be from the same line. "What if it doesn't work?"

"We'll just have to do it without the help."

"And what if it doesn't wear off?"

He thought for a moment. "It should. Though the text I read didn't really talk about its effects on Elves. I would assume it would be the same as poisons—what would kill a human simply makes us sick. So it stands to reason whatever effect the potions have would last less time for us, so we should be quick about it."

And there it was, the evidence that we were related. The willingness to just try something spontaneously and figure it out if things went wrong.

"Seems like a gamble," I said, "but I'll go with it."

"I figured you would." He chuckled. "They shouldn't take me long to prepare once we have the ingredients."

I nodded, blew out a few smoke rings and watched them twist around each other as they rose into the air as we both sat back to wait for Zandra. My mind wandered to Helio. He said he was a student at the college. Based on that fact alone, I would assume that he would know Minoma and its frequenters well, but he seemed too confident in this "unpredictable" crew, too ready to suggest them right away. I didn't want to suspect him, couldn't quite let the thought solidify in my mind, but I felt it nag as Zandra returned with the ingredients and Peverell got to work mixing the potions.

The room filled with an acrid, herby scent as Peverell brewed his concoctions over the fireplace. I hoped the smell wasn't wafting through the entire inn, risking us getting thrown out. Zandra and I stayed close to the window in hopes that our clothes wouldn't absorb the terrible scent.

Once night fell and the potions were bottled, we got ready to leave. Peverell and I dressed as darkly as we could, aiming to blend into the shadows of the bookshelves, our gray skin helping immensely with this task. Zandra left before Pev and I, making her way to the Paramour house she'd previously been employed at.

"You ready for this?" I asked Peverell. He was fussing with his clothes, trying to make sure his face was covered by the shadow of the hood. The last thing we needed was for people to recognize us, though I suspected I had more chance of it than he did.

"Ready as I'll ever be." He looked over himself once more in the mirror before focusing on my reflection and shaking his head. "You can still see your gills, let me help." He turned to face me and none-too-gently adjusted my hood. When that wasn't enough, he removed the tie from around his own neck and wrapped it gently around my own, fussing with the fabric until it was stretched all the way from collar to jaw bone. "There," he said, lowering his shaking hands.

I smirked. "You nervous?"

He laughed. "You're not?"

"This is just another day to me," I lied, slapping his shoulder. "Let's get this over with."

CHAPTER

18

Peverell and I darted through the shadows of the town toward the tower. The library stood atop a cliff that lined the coast, the sound of the waves crashing against the shore welcoming us as we drew closer. Two guards stood at the entry, the two heavy wooden doors solidly shut behind them. Most of the many windows that covered the tower were lit, but there were still many that were darkened.

Peverell's fingers tapped nervously on the trunk of the tree we were squatting behind. "They could be bedrooms," he whispered, "or offices."

"Have you not visited the library before?" I hissed back.

"Years ago, but who's to say they haven't moved things around?"

I looked back at the tower. "That one there," I said, pointing to a window on the first floor. "It's just out of view of the guards."

"What if it's occupied?"

"We won't know unless we investigate." I grunted as I rose from my squat and turned to walk through the darkness.

We walked a bit away from the building before diverting back to it once more, now in the blind spot of the guards. I pressed my face against the window, cupping my hands around my eyes so I could better see the inside. The room was set up as an office; a desk sat directly beneath the window and a small bookshelf lined the wall by the door. I tapped on the glass lightly to see if it stirred up any movement within, but when there was no response. I pulled my knife out, wedged it between the upper and lower window pane, and began teasing the window latch.

"Come on, you fuck," I hissed as I wiggled my knife to and fro, attempting to undo the latch. I kept getting close, but just as it would almost reach the other side, the latch would snap back into the locked position.

"Here, let me," Peverell said, shouldering me out of the way.

"If I can't do it, I highly dou—" The lock clicked. "How did you do that?!"

"Shh!" He hissed, slipping a small knife back into his pocket. "Have you always been this self-absorbed?" he said as he pushed the window quietly up in its frame.

I rolled my eyes and followed him through the window, careful not to knock anything off the desk.

The room was clean and clearly still in regular use, but thankfully empty of anything living. Along one of the sidewalls that I couldn't see through the window was a shelf full of jars with preserved creatures in them. Most contained ordinary beings; lizards, snakes, rodents, but others had two-headed lambs, six-legged kittens, and other things that I didn't want to speculate on.

"All right, let's see if these potions work," I said, turning away to face Peverell. He was still crouched on the desk, fussing with the window. "Will you just leave it?" I hissed.

"I think I broke it," he hissed back.

"We don't have time for this, Pev!"

"Fine." He said, finally sliding off the desk and opening his satchel to pull out his bottled concoctions.

I already knew how terribly they smelt and part of me had hoped that they would at least be appetizing colors, but both brews were an unappealing shade of brown. Peverell handed me two vials and held two of his own.

"Well, bottoms up," he said before closing his eyes and downing the brown liquids in one gulp.

I let out a breath before undoing the lids and pouring the contents down my throat. It took a moment for the flavor to hit me. When it did, I almost gagged—just as Peverell did beside me.

"Fuck, Pev, you couldn't make them taste better?" I choked. But I instantly forgot about the taste as I watched my brother's form slowly fade before my eyes. I held up my own hands and froze as I watched them disappear just as Peverell's had, the walls lined with dead things in jars becoming more and more visible through them with each passing moment. "Mother's pit, you did it, Peverell!"

"I'm honestly surprised it worked," he said with a chuckle. "We must hurry though. It won't last long.

If he moved after saying that, I didn't know, because as I moved myself it was followed by no sound. Even the rustle of my clothes was silent. I watched as my foot fell and was met with nothing but the sensation of touch.

"Pev," I hissed, "Where are you?"

"Here." His voice came from beside me.

I jumped, my heart thundering in my chest. "You scared the shit out of me!"

"Yes, this could be a problem," he conceded. "I'm going to touch you, try not to scream."

I couldn't stop myself from flinching as I felt his hand move past my face and land on my shoulder soundlessly. It was so unnerving to feel something happen with no warning of any kind.

"We can't sneak around like this," I said in what I imagined was his general direction.

"You take the top, I'll take the bottom?"

"Sounds fair. Scream if you need me."

He laughed and, with that, removed his hand from my shoulder. I tried to step toward the door and crashed into him. Rather than argue about it, I pushed him toward the door and waited to move until I saw it open and close again.

My lungs and legs burned as I topped the sixth or seventh flight of stairs. I was cautious when I first left the first floor office, but after coming face to face with a mage and them remaining completely oblivious to my presence, I felt more confident. I bent over, my hands resting on my knees at the top of the stairs, breathing deeply. If I stopped going up now, I knew I would not continue after scouting this floor. I had to get to the top and work my way down. Worse than the exertion was the heat.

Despite the sun being completely set and the moon high in the sky, the inside of the tower was uncomfortably hot. Sweat slid down my back and soaked into the waistband of my pants, which rubbed irritatingly on my torso.

"All right," I whispered to myself and continued my journey up the many sets of stairs.

When I reached the top, a significant amount of time had passed; I was physically exhausted and drenched in sweat. I was surprised to see that there wasn't a trail of sweat droplets following my every step, despite the excessive amount that coated my body. I used the sweat on my forehead to pull my hair back from my face. I couldn't see it, but I could feel the strands tickling my nose and sticking to the sides of my face.

It seemed most of the humans were sleeping, but there were a few night-owls stalking the isles of books, some quietly studying others, muttering to themselves as they paced, sometimes stopping to jot something down on a roll of parchment. I scoured the top floor but found mostly outdated tomes and irrelevant artifacts, it seemed to mostly be used as a storage and maintenance level. Ladders and planks of wood were stacked by the edge of the balconies; I could only assume they were used to reach the ties for the gigantic skeleton that hung down the center of the structure. Everyone who saw it probably marveled at its size, thinking it the biggest sea creature to ever be seen, but I knew this was practically a newborn compared to the size of the beasts I'd met.

I worked my way back down the tower, checking each floor thoroughly while not wasting too much time on each level. The closer to the middle I got, the more active the mages were. It became increasingly more difficult to avoid almost running into people—more than once I had to stop a bookcase from tumbling over after skidding to a halt mere inches away from a mage walking with their face buried in a book. It was also becoming more and more disorientating not being able to see my own body, to not be able to tell if I was at risk of hitting something with my hip or my shoulder. It slowed me down more than I would have thought and only added to my heavy feeling of exhaustion. After climbing so many stairs and scouring at least five floors, all I wanted to do was collapse into one of the small, cushioned alcoves and sleep. But, as I hobbled down to the next floor, I noticed my boot make a slight tap as it hit the uncarpeted stone.

"Shit," I murmured to myself.

We were running out of time.

I pushed through the discomfort and pain and darted through the level as fast as I could before moving on to the next. I wished there was some way that I could contact Peverell, but I was scared to even breathe too loudly. My pulse was racing in my ears, my heart itself about to explode out of my chest. I hoped he was safe, that he hadn't gotten himself caught—or slacked off and been distracted by some rare book.

I could tell I was getting closer to where the map piece could be just based off the books lining the shelves. So many of them were about the fall of the fairies and the introduction of elves to Carynthia, the loss of goblin magic.

"Come on, come on," I chanted to myself as I searched the level, scanned the bookshelves, snuck into closed offices, but still, I found nothing. I was beginning to become frustrated and less cautious. A trail of books littered the floor in my wake as I made my way through two more floors, my footsteps making more and more noise as I went. This wasn't meant to take so long, we were meant to be in and out as fast as possible, but it was beginning to feel as if I would be here all night, and with the potion wearing off I could be caught at any moment. I could only hope that Pev—

I froze on the stairwell down to the next floor as a bang rang up from the first floor before quickly ducking behind the banister as mages from all over the tower began to flood the balconies.

A chorus of "What was that?" echoed down around me, and I used the excess of noise to mask my steps as I darted back up to the floor I'd been leaving so I could hide among the bookshelves. I could hear chaos ensuing on the lower floors and could only guess that Peverell had alerted Zandra.

I risked moving to the edge of the balcony so I could glance over the balustrade. Dancers were streaming in through the library entrance as confused mages huddled around them in a semicircle. There was no way I could have heard what was being said, but even from this distance I could spot the ever-familiar gestures of "What do you think you're doing?!" and "We did not ask for this!".

A hand clasped down on my shoulder and before I could even consider that it could be my brother, I'd gripped it, twisted, and pulled a knife.

"Bellona!" Peverell gasped. "It's me, you idiot."

"You're the fucking idiot!" I hissed back, releasing his arm. "Why would you sneak up on me like that?!"

"Well, I couldn't really announce myself, could I?" He bit back. "I've got the map—"

"Oh, thank fuck! Let's get the pit out of here," I said, reaching for his arm and pulling him toward the stairs.

"Bell." He pulled us back into the line of bookshelves and held our hazy hands before my eyes. "We're becoming visible again."

I groaned. "Of course we are." We were still barely visible, little more than figures made of a thin fog, but how long would it be before the potion fully wore off? "How do we do this, then?"

"I don't know." Peverell whined. "Stick to the shadows?"

I rolled my eyes but proceeded with that in mind.

Thanks to the dancers, the majority of the mages were distracted and the others expertly ignoring the display—and, by extension, us. We slid down the stairs as silently as possible, sticking as close to the walls as we could and crouching in the shadows when we had to. If anyone noticed us and thought us anything more than a few stray spirits, they kept it to themselves.

We managed to get to the first floor before we were mostly visible, our forms now more smoke-like than fog. I met the eyes of some of the dancers, who must have been told to look out for us, and found that they quickly swept us up in a blur of skirts, capes, and scarves. Under the cover of the flowing garments and flailing dancers, we were able to escape the tower completely unnoticed.

CHAPTER
19

Peverell and I stayed on high alert until we were safely back in our room at the tavern, the potions completely worn off. Peverell straight away sat before the table with the map in front of him and began translating, while I packed everything as fast as I could so we could leave before the mages caught on that they'd been robbed. The sun was rising and with it the sound of the dancers making their way back through the city, music following them as they went.

"You're not going to like this, Bell," Peverell muttered as he jotted down a note in his book.

"What?" I asked, moving to stand beside him and looking down at the map.

He pointed the end of his quill at the map. It depicted the northern third of Carynthia, Kushyam, Minoma, Osiria, and the island above. "It's there," Peverell said, tapping the island shown above Osiria. "Somewhere on that island is an entrance to an old Goblin Queendom."

"Somewhere?"

"I haven't translated the coordinates yet."

"They had coordinates?" I was dumbfounded. I had always thought elves had brought that knowledge over with us.

"Where do you think we learned it from?" Peverell laughed, "The elves that came here knew nothing but how to fight. That's why the fairies brought them over. The goblins had knowledge that surpasses even what we have now, and their enchanting magic is still unparalleled," he gushed. "It is a shame the Mother and Father took it from them."

The door to the room burst open and Zandra stormed in, already stripping her dancers' clothes. "We have to get the *fuck* out of here," she said urgently.

"What's happened?" I asked, scooping up Peverell's things and stuffing them in a bag, being careful to leave out the used quill and open bottle of ink.

"The Head Mage got involved. No one's hurt or anything, but she demanded the tower be searched."

"Damn academics! Can never appreciate a good party." I swung a couple of bags over my shoulders and moved to the door. "I'm leaving now. I'll not risk this whole thing crumbling down, not when we're so close."

"Wait!" Peverell threw his hand out to stop me. "I don't want you going alone with him."

"Peverell, this is not the time to play big brother."

"I'm not playing 'big brother', I'm playing interested party who doesn't want to miss out on his cut."

"I'll bring your cut to you, but I'm leaving now."

"Bellona! Please, I don't trust him."

"Fine." I said, adjusting my hold on the bags and ignoring the stab of guilt at what I was about to do. "I'm going to the docks—if you're not there in twenty minutes, we leave without you."

Peverell spun and began packing his satchel. Zandra glanced at me, her hand resting on a dagger at her hip. I tilted my head to the side and before I could blink she'd pulled it out and hit Peverell in the head with the butt. I ignored the twist in my gut as Peverell crumpled to the ground in a heap and, together, we lifted him from the ground and placed him on one of the beds.

"He's going to be pissed when he wakes up," I warned Zandra as I flicked a stray hair from Peverell's face. "Just make sure he gets back to The Siren. He knows where I'm headed, but don't let him come after me until you're with the others." She nodded and I rose to leave, first double-checking that I had everything I needed, including Peverell's notebook and the map piece.

"Captain," Zandra said just as I was reaching for the door handle. "I do agree with your brother—that Osirian …there's something going on with him."

I nodded and left the room.

The docks were full of activity, making it easy enough for me to blend in with the crowds—not that I'd noticed any mages out hunting for thieves—but it made finding Helio difficult. The Minoman port was huge; it needed to be with how much cargo came in and out of the city, especially the size of the cargo. Barrels the size of carts were stacked along the docks and filled nearby storehouses, filled themselves with fermenting grapes or freshly made wine.

I strolled down the docks, past the large cargo ships and only slightly smaller passenger vessels, and entered the market area of the port. Smaller ships are docked here for transporting smaller cargo, fishing boats weaving between them seamlessly—much like the small fish they catch, darting between families of whales.

I decided to take a moment to walk through the market stalls, appraising the wares, before I was to once again climb aboard a ship. I loved to be at sea, but it was nice to come on land every now and then, and recently I'd felt I hadn't had a chance to truly enjoy that time.

As I walked through the stalls I began to feel eyes on me, I was used to the attention when my gills were visible, but they were currently hidden beneath a scarf. I looked around me, disguising my suspicion as someone trying to tell the time by the position of the sun, but I could spot no one that seemed to be going out of their way to watch me. As I proceeded down the docks, I continued to feel someone's heavy gaze, but no matter how many times I stopped to check around me, I never spotted anyone.

I was just about to leave the market area when I felt a light tug on one of my bags. Without thinking, I turned with my fist raised and it connected solidly with the face of the person I thought had been trying to steal from me.

"*Shit.*" Helio groaned as blood poured from his nose.

"Well, that's what you get for sneaking up on me," I said, shaking my hand, my knuckles aching slightly. "Why didn't you just come straight to me?"

"*Hello? Osirian,*" Helio gestured to himself with one hand as the other held his shirt to his nose, using it to soak up the blood. "Just because you're comfortable around me, doesn't mean others are," he said resentfully.

"Of course," I said apologetically, reaching up to heal his nose with my magic. Blue mist spread across his face from my outstretched hand, the color also reflected in his white hair, hidden beneath a hood. "I take it you were the one following me."

He dropped his hand and shirt. "Sorry, I can't quite walk around freely without causing a mass evacuation."

"Fair enough," I said, ceasing my magic as the blood dried beneath his nose.

Helio took my wrist before I could lower my hand and kissed my palm. "Thank you."

"I was the one who caused it, I don't think you should thank me."

"Shouldn't I?" he murmured, slipping his tongue between my fingers and sending a shiver rippling down my spine.

I grinned. "Thank me later," I said. "For now, we need to get out of here."

Helio looked disappointed but agreed and led me to the ship. It was a two-masted brigantine called *The Maiden*. It was nothing much to look at, painted a deep navy, its sails resembling patchwork blankets more than functional canvas, and its figurehead of a woman was missing half its face.

"It's not the best-looking ship, but it's unassuming, and the crew agreed to our terms," Helio said before leading me up the gangplank. "They're also the only crew that would speak to me," he added, and once we reached the main deck I understood why.

The crew was almost completely made up of Osirians, their white hair stark against the blue of the Minoman sky, and the rest were Kushyami with a few stray Minomans.

"Is this all right?" Helio asked, gently running a finger down the back of my hand.

"Yeah, it's fine," I said, pushing forward and stepping onto the deck.

"Mr. Lothar!" called the Captain from the small quarter-deck. "Are we casting off?"

Helio glanced at me. I nodded and, despite his confused expression, he confirmed with the Captain to cast off and led me down into a small room with nothing but a cot inside. "What happened? Where's Peverell?"

"Peverell's fine, I just didn't want him to come along for this part," I said dispassionately.

"This is quite possibly the worst time for you to not bring him along," Helio said harshly, slumping down on the edge of the cot. "We need him to translate everything! Couldn't you have a sibling squabble after we'd finished the job?"

I leaned against the wall behind me. "We're not having a squabble. I didn't want him dragging me down, and it's really none of your fucking business," I replied sharply, not wanting to stew in my guilt anymore than I already was.

"Do you even know where we're meant to be going?"

"Osiria," I said, pulling out the map and my brother's notebook and throwing them on the cot beside him. "I wouldn't have left him if I didn't think we could do it without him. I'm not a fucking idiot, Helio."

Helio snatched up the notebook and flattened the map across the bed, scoffing lightly at my comment. "I don't think you're an idiot, just prone to being rash."

"Well, I decided to go against everyone else's beliefs and trust you." I threw back, crossing my arms over my chest.

The challenge dropped from his shoulders. "I'm sorry. I'm just—I know how this will reflect on you. Having others with us protected you from that."

"You think I care?" I laughed. "My reputation was already squandered long before I met you."

"I'm just the cherry on top, am I? The last rebellion for the disgraced Carracallan Princess?"

"If you say so." I shrugged, no energy left to continue the argument.

Exhaustion crashed into me like a tidal wave, and all I wanted to do was push Helio and the maps off the cot and sleep. I'd ignored my aching legs since escaping the tower, but now, leaning against the wall of the ship, the pain was almost unbearable. I doubted I'd be able to walk even after resting. And my mind wouldn't shut up. It had decided that now was the perfect time to run through every single reason leaving Peverell behind was a bad idea, why traveling with a crew of Osirians was a bad idea, why this whole quest was a bad idea.

Helio seemed to read my mind. As he began gathering the many things scattered over the bed, he said, "I'm going to inform the Captain of our heading and continue working on deck, I'm not quite ready to be back below deck for the gods know how long. You get some rest." He added, moving past me to the door, brushing his fingers along mine as he went. It sent a jolt through me that I hadn't felt in years, decades even. A jolt that I shouldn't be feeling, that I'd been denying, but was now too tired to pretend wasn't there.

I let out a sigh as the door clicked shut and flopped onto the cot. Relief was instantaneous, but if I moved, even slightly, to get more comfortable the tightness and pain returned, so I remained flat on my stomach, my face buried in the pillow. As I succumbed to exhaustion, my mind conjured dreams of a life with Helio, a pleasant distraction from its previous line of thought. Happy moments aboard my ship, even happier moments on land, and then small moments of betrayal until they all climaxed into a nightmare. My black soul being ripped from my body when I should have been in a state of ecstasy, and my death leading Helio to his.

CHAPTER
20

Sailing to the island north of Osiria seemed to take no time at all, almost like time was slipping away now that we were approaching the end of our journey. I'd spent most of it in the small cabin Helio and I shared, not really wanting to hang about on deck with a crew of Osirians. One was fine, even a couple or three, but a whole crew, more than ten? It was too many. They brought on too many memories I'd worked hard to force down into the deep depths of my mind. Without the dull of alcohol to keep them there, I feared they'd creep to the surface with no familiar face to help me bury them back down. I wondered if there would ever be a time that I would be free of the torment.

Helio had been in and out of the cabin for the whole journey. He seemed to have a whole new air of confidence about him since being around his own people. It put into perspective, to a degree, how he must have felt on my ship and *The Duat*, lonely and other, as I felt now.

I couldn't blame them for staring the few times I'd left the cabin, having given up on hiding my identity; it was not normal for them to see someone with gills, it wasn't really normal for anyone outside my family and crew. I was relatively used to the attention, but wary of who it was coming from. Sometimes I couldn't tell if the crew were fascinated with me or sizing me up to sell me to the highest bidder.

There were collectors, such as Ikram, who collected strange creatures and would pay a hefty sum if it meant possessing the last gilled Carracallan. It had been a fear of mine for a long time that that would be how I'd meet my end, but now I almost welcomed the person brave enough to try it.

Helio crashed through the cabin door, waving the map above his head as he stumbled over to the cot where I lay.

"I've done it!" He said triumphantly. "I've translated the coordinates and located the city!" He dropped the map onto my lap, barely waiting for me to sit up to properly inspect it before jabbing a finger at it. "There. The entrance is there, hidden somehow for thousands of years!"

"A city?" I asked, examining the spot he'd pinpointed on the map.

"Beneath the ground," he said, bouncing onto the cot before me.

"How do you know?"

"It's written beneath the coordinates. I thought perhaps it would be a tomb to the Queen, or an old palace, but it's a whole city!" He sighed. "Peverell would have loved to see it."

"Yeah, yeah, I'm a terrible sister," I said, staring down at the map. There was nothing to show an entrance, or even that a city existed on the island, just a small bit of goblin text scrawled in the corner of the torn page. I'd expected something slightly more grand, but I suppose that would defeat the purpose of a secret location on a secret map.

Without warning, Helio snatched the map from my hands and threw it on the ground. Then he pushed me down and pinned me against the worn pillow of the cot, his hands on either side of my head, an unfamiliar glint in his eye.

"I've been waiting for this for such a long time," he said, dipping his face to my neck and running his nose up the length of my throat and jaw, sending a jolt of arousal through me. His lips met mine in a crushing kiss, our teeth knocking together uncomfortably before we corrected. He kissed along my jaw as his hands moved to run down my torso.

"Years I've been searching for that fucking map," he whispered in my ear, taking the lobe between his teeth in a quick nip. "Now, we have it. Now we know where it is," he continued, grinding against me. Our mouths came together again, but we couldn't seem to match rhythms as we normally did. It was as if his mind were somewhere else, as if he were someone else, dancing to a different beat.

I wasn't shy to a switch up of dynamics in the bedroom, but something felt wrong, different. My mind took me back to our first conversation in my cabin, the way his anger had so quickly spiked at my false accusation of him being a deserter. That was the Helio I was dealing with now, the same fierce passion. The arousal I'd first felt turned to something bordering fear.

"Helio," I pleaded, and not in the way he wanted.

He paused, his face going almost blank. He rose off me, resting back on his heels. "Sorry. I ... I was just caught up in the moment."

"It's fine," I deflected, sitting up. "You just ... you seemed different."

Helio seemed to recoil at my words, as if I'd slapped him, but recovered quickly. "Sorry, I suppose I'm just excited." He slowly reached out to run a finger through my hair. I let him. "I've been dreaming about finding this place for decades and now that we've found it ... I guess I just lost myself," he said, but almost more to himself than to me, his eyes fixed on the hand he ran through my hair. "I didn't mean to make you uncomfortable."

"It's fine," I dismissed, grasping for another reason for my withdrawal. "I suppose it's finally hitting me that I deserted my brother, when he would have been just as excited as you."

Helio responded with a sympathetic hum before pulling me against his body in a tight hug. "You'll just have to come back with him," he said, stroking my hair.

"Only if he stops being such a pain in my arse."

"A pain in your arse, or a pain in Jarrel's?"

I groaned in disgust against his chest. "I'd almost forgotten about that!" I whined.

Helio laughed, "I'm sorry. I couldn't help myself."

I flopped down onto the cot, staring up at the wooden ceiling of the cabin. "How long till we reach the goblin city?"

"A day or two," Helio said.

I sighed. "More waiting."

"Only a little more—then the fun begins," he said, leaning over and patting my thigh before rising from the bed. "I'll bring you dinner. Or will you come and eat on deck?"

"I'll come eat on deck," I said after a moment's pause. "I need to get out of this room."

He smiled and left, gently closing the door behind himself.

I let out a breath and massaged my eyes. I was sick of the waiting, sick of how long everything was taking. Had I gone on this journey alone, I'd have been done with it by now. I could swim much faster than a ship could sail, and had more allies below the sea than above it. These last few months could have been only weeks. A voice somewhere deep in the back of my mind whined that I wouldn't have met Helio had it not been for my slow journey, but I had a feeling that we would have crossed paths eventually, and time was yet to tell if meeting him had been good in the first place.

A cool wind whipped through my hair as I joined the crew on the upper deck for dinner, and a bowl of some kind of soup was placed in my hands. I crossed the deck to join Helio, who was leaning against the bulwark, spooning the gelatinous soup into his mouth as he stared intently at the island before us. It was exactly like Osiria, practically split down the middle, one side volcanic, the other icy. Small patches of green scattered the island. I guessed they would have been areas where the goblins would have grown food. I wondered if there were any crops left, if they had survived unattended for so long.

It was odd to view the location of a journey's end when it still seemed there was so much journey to be had. But the second we stepped onto that island, it would be the beginning of the end, and there was still much left for me to consider. Would I share the prize or keep it to myself? Would Helio be satisfied with viewing it and leaving it in my possession? Would whatever was going on between us continue, or were we both just a means to an end for each other? Did he care? I glanced over at him. He didn't seem to have noticed my presence at all, his eyes still fixed on the island, his mind somewhere else once again.

I cleared my throat before speaking. "So, that's it, is it?"

"That's it," Helio said monotonously. "How frustrating to think I was so close all this time. I must have sailed past this island thousands of times in my life.

We even landed there a few times while I was in the navy." He paused for a moment, dropping his spoon down into his half-finished soup. "To think I was there, on the island with it, completely unaware."

"Happens to the best of us," I jested.

A smile crept across his face, as if my joke had pulled him from his trance. "Are you feeling well?" he asked.

"Yes. The rest I've managed to have on this leg has been very healing. I hadn't realized how much I needed it."

"Good. I have a feeling our excursion onto the island won't be an easy one, especially not through the ruins."

"Surely, there won't be anyone left?"

"You can never be sure. If it's not a hidden goblin horde, it'll be what's left of the other island inhabitants—and Mother knows what kind of traps the goblins could have left."

"More traps?" I groaned, mouth full of soup. From the flavor, I guessed it was some kind of fish.

"Of course," Helio said, almost laughing. "The goblins were incredible craftspeople and, before the war, enchanters. I've heard tales of troll-like creatures completely made of stone."

"How do you kill stone?"

"That's the point," he said, a little too excitedly. "You can't."

"Marvelous," I managed while pinning a lump of potato to the roof of my mouth with my tongue.

"It's not too late to turn back, Princess."

I swallowed the potato whole. "I'm not turning back now," I said sternly. "I'm seeing this through, otherwise all this time will have been wasted."

"All of it?" Helio asked, meeting my gaze.

"I suppose it depends."

"On what?"

"On how it ends," I said, my gaze scanning across the ship, the crew, and the island before us. Helio hummed in what I took as agreement and left to speak to the Captain. I watched them as I ate the remainder of my soup. It looked to be a normal interaction, a passenger inquiring into something to do with the journey or the ship, but the dispositions seemed reversed. I would have expected the Captain to hold some authority over Helio, but she seemed to subdue herself in his presence, and he held himself higher. I wouldn't have thought anything of it, had I not known his past. Anyone with naval training would recognize the Captain as their superior when aboard their ship, and Helio's blatant disregard for hierarchy made me uneasy.

I scanned the crew, keeping my face as neutral as possible. Some had finished their meals and were settling in for the night. Others sat together still drinking and eating. As my eyes scanned over them, I noticed that many turned their faces away. It was subtle enough that if I hadn't been looking for it, I wouldn't have noticed, but it fanned the flame of distrust in me, and I had to remind myself that we were at sea. If anyone could escape from a ship safely at sea, it was me.

Collecting my bowl with forced casualness, I cleaned it in a barrel of dirty water before adding it to the pile of others—all of them still glistening with residual oil from the soup—and returned to my room. I made sure to fasten the lock and then kept a knife by my side for the remainder of the journey.

CHAPTER
21

The boat rocked on the waves as a selection of the crew rowed us to shore. Helio and I had spoken with the captain, Adra, about who was best to accompany us. She'd recommended a delicately framed Kushyami woman, with locs that almost reached the backs of her knees; three giant Osirian men, their white hair cut at different lengths—the one with the longest hair looked as if he could crush my head between his hands with little effort; and a Minoman, who seemed more happy to be heading to land than they'd ever seemed on the ship. We'd brought them and another boat of Osirians at Helio's behest. I felt out-numbered, but also comforted by their presence. Their death magic could come in handy if we attracted any unsavory attention.

As we came to shore, everyone leapt out of the boats and dragged them up onto the beach, far enough up the sand that the tide shouldn't reach them when it came in. At first, I wasn't sure it was safe to leave the boat. The sand beneath my feet was black as the smoke rising from the volcano to the west, but Helio reassured me that it was fine—there were no pit creatures lying in wait beneath the grains. I scanned the sparse horizon. There was almost a completely uninterrupted view of the whole island, only small patches of greenery and the odd hill blocked the view of the shore on the opposite side.

I was again hit with a pang of regret for having left Peverell behind. I wished he could have experienced the odd feeling this island had. The air was a strange mix of hot and cold that sometimes smelled of salt from the sea, snow from the icy side of the island, or carried the rancid smell of the volcanoes. Only adding to my feelings of betrayal was the sight of Helio carrying my brother's notebook and using it to navigate and decipher the map. With the notebook in hand and numerous bags filled with unnecessary items such as paper, quills and charcoal, I could almost imagine that Helio was possessed by the spirit of my brother.

As Helio led the party north-east, I trailed along behind, lost in thought and memories. I wondered if Eevan was regretting not joining us, if he'd even thought of me as he sat in his palace with his wife and daughter, or was he content? Would I ever find that? Someone to settle down with, to be content with? Someone I'd be willing to put my life of adventure aside for? The part of my mind that still longed for whorehouses and spirits scoffed at the thought, but the sober, sensible side of me silently hoped for a time of quiet. Perhaps after this adventure, I would return home, to Carracalla, and stay for a few years, or decades. Peverell could take my ship and crew, be with Jarrel, and hunt for the many goblin ruins scattered around Carynthia.

"Bellona!" Helio called from the front of the party, pulling me from my thoughts. I jogged up to meet him.

He smiled as he pointed forward. "There it is," he said, beaming. "The entrance."

He'd gestured to a mammoth rock. Not a mountain or a hill—just one large, round stone that stood at least the height of three masts. Carved into its face was an archway. From a distance I couldn't tell what it was made up of, but as we grew closer I could see familiar runes and depictions of day-to-day goblin life … and death. We'd been surprised to learn that it wasn't just a tomb we were looking for but a city, but these carvings seemed to allude to it being a city of the dying and dead.

It appeared as if the goblins would send their ill and aged here to live out the remainder of their lives before then being entombed within. A practice that at first seemed odd, but as I thought about it more, it made perfect sense. We fear not knowing where we will end up when we die, where our bodies will be put to rest, but these people knew, they lived there and maintained it themselves. If they were not happy with where they ended up after they passed, they would return here and it would be their own fault if it were not to their standard.

"How do we get in?" I asked. There was no obvious opening, no slit in the stone or concealed door in the ground, just carvings in the rock face.

Helio ran a hand over the carvings, his eyes trailing over them as he translated them in his mind, only referencing Peverell's notes once or twice. He chewed his bottom lip as he read and sighed as he finally turned to face me. "It's not going to be good … or particularly easy."

"Go on," I urged.

"Well, given what kind of place this was, to gain entry one must be close to death."

"And what exactly does that mean?" demanded the Kushyami woman, her hazel eyes locked on Helio and I.

"Is anyone here ill? Or injured? Aged?" asked Helio.

The party cast quizzical glances at each other, some inspected themselves as if wounds would magically appear on their limbs.

"We could make someone close to death," the large Osirian with short hair suggested, a menacing smile creeping across his face as he eyed the paling Minoman.

I rolled my eyes and stepped forward. "Helio, were these ruins constructed before or after the blessing of the elves?" I asked, already assuming the answer was before.

"Before the blessing. Why?"

"If that's the case, then I would assume they'd not been built with Osirian magic in mind. Is there anything closer to death than that?"

Helio considered this for a moment before summoning his power, his hand becoming lost in a black haze that seemed impossibly dark in the bright afternoon sun. I resisted the urge to shrink away from his magic, fought against my every instinct to cower or fight. He reached up with his hand and hesitated only a moment before touching it to the rock face.

The ground beneath our feet began to shake. There was a chorus of unsure exclamations as the party tried to keep themselves balanced as the ground groaned and shook beneath us. Without thinking, I reached out and clung to Helio's shoulder, my fingers knotting in the fabric of his shirt.

Before our eyes, the rock face split down the center and began to separate, creating a doorway. Dust and crumbling rock rained down toward us from where the rock ground against itself after Mother and Father knows how long of it not moving.

Once the dust cleared, I gazed down at Helio's face; it was bright with excitement, but that glint lurked behind his eyes once more, though I could tell he was trying to keep it hidden. I glanced away, not wanting to dwell on it when we were finally at the end of our journey.

I looked up at the great doorway that had opened before us and, despite my amazement, couldn't help but scoff a little. Most of the goblins I had met had barely reached the height of my knee, yet the doorway was large enough for even the biggest sea beasts. Typical.

I took a tentative step forward, but Helio pulled me back, his hand whipping to my wrist faster than I could catch it.

He called the Minoman forward and ordered them to step through the archway. Their curiosity must have won out over the cowardly nature they'd presented so far because they took the orders and stepped forward with only the barest hesitation. The party collectively held their breath, not understanding what was going on— I didn't understand myself at first. I glanced sidelong at Helio to find his face stern and studying as the Minoman continued to move slowly through the massive door, and it was then I remembered the warning of traps. The truth of what was happening crashed home in my mind as the Minoman passed through to the other side.

They stood still for a moment, as if they also expected something to happen. When nothing did, they shrugged and waved for the rest of us to join. Relief surged through me, but Helio's hand tightened on my wrist before I could move, signaling for me to stay where I was just as a pop and hiss echoed through the cavern beyond.

The Minoman was skewered before my warning could leave my lips.

A line of spikes had shot up from the floor and now lined the base of the opening. The Minoman had been standing just beyond them, but close enough that they were now dead with a spike protruding from the top of their skull. Bone fragments, blood, and parts of their brain rained down around them in a soft shower. I was suddenly extremely grateful that Peverell was not here, after all.

"Now we can move forward," Helio said in a commanding voice, loud enough for everyone to hear.

"How do you know there's not more traps?" one of the large Osirians demanded.

"Oh, there is. That's why you're all going first." Helio turned to look at the group of sailors, as if daring any of them to challenge him. None did so verbally, but the Osirian squared his shoulders. "I've paid your Captain a rather handsome sum for your services. Would you disappoint her by not following my orders? Because either way, you may end up dead."

I did my best to hide the shock that rattled through me at Helio's words, but did nothing to contradict them. I would have ordered the same thing, had I arranged the crew and paid the Captain, but I never would have thought Helio would do the same. But hadn't I just seen him send a person to their death? He'd wanted this for so long, he'd told me as much. I should have assumed it had gotten to the point of doing whatever it took. I suppose part of me had hoped he would be better than I and if he wasn't, hadn't been this whole time … what else had he done in pursuit of this treasure? How many bodies had he left in his wake? The Shinchaku temple flashed in my mind, the bodies scattered across the trapped floor …

We stood and waited together for the rest of the party to enter the ruins before us, studying which paths they took and whether or not they tripped any more traps. Once they were all through, we followed.

The air inside the cavern was dank and heavy, drips and the occasional scurrying were the only sounds echoing throughout the vast space. The ceiling above us glittered as the sunlight caught the stalactites, but not enough to distract from what lay before us.

The ground of the cavern was littered with bones, small and delicate, coated in the worthless crystals that form in caves. We stood, all of us staring over the cave floor, realizing that every little raised bit, every bump on the road was a skull, a pelvis, a piece of something that had once been living.

There were so many bumps on the road …

"It was a massacre," Helio said quietly, but loud enough that everyone heard it. "They were sick and already dying, but they still took the time to kill them all."

"Who did?" I asked.

"The first Carynthian Elves. The ones brought over by the fairies."

"That would have been before Osirian magic," I said, and took a moment to let it sink in. These sick and dying goblins hadn't been swiftly killed with magic, they'd been slaughtered with hands and weapons. I doubted anyone within our party was innocent of killing, I had killed more than I could ever remember in times of war, and yet we all stood in silent horror.

"No point wasting our energy on it now," I said bluntly when it was clear no one else was willing to move us forward. "We can't change what's been done." I stepped forward and resisted the urge to flinch as my boot crunched through a tiny skull.

There was murmured agreement, torches were lit, and then the sound of drips and scurrying were joined by a chorus of bones crunching beneath our feet.

CHAPTER
22

The crunching of bones beneath our boots continued the whole way through the first level of the city until we were numb to it. Someone recommended relocating the bodies rather than walking over them, but most of them were fused to the ground by stalagmites and crystal growths, the others so fragile that lifting them damaged them as much as walking on them did.

The cavern had become home for a surprising number of creatures; lizards, goats, and deer, ones that had survived the massacre and others that naturally inhabited the island. We disturbed them occasionally, their frantic escapes only adding to the echoing crack of bones. There must have been another opening in the cavern that they were able to get in through.

The deeper we delved into the cavern, the wetter and warmer the air became until some were finding it difficult to breathe and we had to stop and rest. Each time we stopped, Helio would pace or fidget endlessly.

"Can we move yet?" he demanded.

"Just a little longer, I can barely catch my breath," gasped the Kushyami girl. I was not at all surprised at her struggling the most—she was used to the dry air of deserts and soft sand beneath her feet, not the harsh uneven stone and bone. I wouldn't have been surprised if she felt like she was drowning in the dense, moist air.

"We can always cut off the dead weight," one of the large Osirians muttered.

I shot him a warning look. I would not put up with unnecessary killing. Purposefully tripping traps to protect the majority was one thing, but killing a girl for struggling to breathe in an unusual environment was not all right with me. "We'll sit for as long as everyone needs," I challenged.

Helio's eyes flicked to mine. There was a flash of anger, but it subsided quickly, his shoulders relaxing as he stopped his pacing and sat on a nearby rock.

I walked over and joined him. "There's no rush," I said in a hushed tone.

"I know," he said, running his hand over his sweat-covered face and through his hair. "It's just so infuriating being *so close* and taking so long."

"I understand, but look at where we are." I gestured to the city of ruin that surrounded us, the small stone houses left in disrepair. "Is this not a scholar's dream?"

Helio gazed around the cavern, a smile slowly creeping across his face. "You're right. I shouldn't take this opportunity so lightly." He rose from the rock. "I'm going to have a look around, yell when you're ready to keep moving."

I nodded and watched him leave, notebook in hand. I cast my gaze across the surrounding area, attempting to inconspicuously eye the crew and see how they acted when Helio was away. They seemed to have separated into groups, one looked to be quite happy chatting between each other and the other was not so inconspicuously eyeing me. I felt their eyes on me as I rose from the rock and moved a short distance away, sizing me up. I had a feeling that if there was any other interested party that we should have been worried about, we'd already brought them with us. I could only hope that Helio would be strong enough to help me take them out before they got us.

A low growl echoed through the cavern, followed by a shout and rapid crunching footsteps.

"Weapons!" I ordered without thinking twice. I pulled out my blade, wishing I had something longer than a cutlass as I spotted the troll thundering toward us behind Helio in the gloom ahead. "Did you have to lead that thing back here?!" I shouted as he skidded to a halt at my side.

"Would you have rathered I died out there alone?"

"Honestly? Yes!" I said as I corrected his hold on his own cutlass.

The torches had been laid on the ground or stuck between rocks to light the area we'd stopped in, and the light cast a flickering glow on the troll that only added to its terrifying figure. It bounded toward us, propelling itself forward with its oversized arms, drool hanging down from its mouth held permanently open by the large canines protruding from its bottom lip.

It snarled as it spotted the rest of us and increased its speed, bones crushing under its large fists as it charged. Helio and I leapt to the side as it closed in and slashed at the troll's arms—it howled in frustration and swung its now bleeding arms up and brought them down onto the floor, sending a rumble through the stone that left all of us unsteady on our feet. It growled again as it flung its arms out and snorted triumphantly as it hit one of the large Osirians in the head. There was a crunch before and after they hit the ground; blood smeared their face and pooled on the ground around their head.

"Someone see to him!" Helio shouted, quickly gesturing to the body on the floor before ducking out of the way of another swinging troll fist.

The creature howled as the Kushyami girl's spear shot through one of its feet and it slipped on its own blood, the thud of its head hitting the floor making the ground shake once again.

"Let us take care of this," one of the remaining large Osirians said as he and the other stepped forward. Looking at them now, I could see the similarities in their faces and realized they were most likely siblings, if not triplets. The two called on their magic and the cavern seemed to grow darker despite the torchlight. Black mist blocked out their hands, their eyes grew black and together they raised their arms, the muscles bulging as if together they were struggling to pull the life out of the troll.

The beast snarled and coughed against the magic, its eyes going wide with fear as it realized there was no point in fighting. The troll coughed and coughed. Each time it did it grew weaker as the Osirians pulled the black remnants of its life force out through its mouth and nose. Eventually, a black cloud filled the air above the creature's body and it was dead.

The presumed brothers dashed over to their third and assisted the couple of Osirians who were working on healing him. Having been around so many Isidians, I'd forgotten how difficult healing was for the rest of us. Now, I almost marveled at the fact that it could take four Osirians to heal a broken nose, but only two to kill a troll.

"Is he all right?" I asked no one in particular.

"Hard to say," replied an Osirian woman I'd seen a few times on the ship, "when we heal we have to wait for the injured to let us know. All our magic can tell us is that they're alive when they should be dead."

I nodded, unsure of what else I could say. It wasn't often that Osirians would talk about their magic, much less talk to outsiders about it, and I didn't want to seem as if I were pushing for information.

"We can't stay here next to that," Helio said, jerking his thumb toward the dead troll. "The smell could bring all kinds of things our way."

Nothing about what he said should have stood out, but the confidence with which he said it sparked something in my mind. It was almost like he knew what would come after us. I couldn't tell if I was justified in my paranoia, or if it was just that. Was this a front or the real Helio? Was the Helio I'd met in Shinchaku a front? The Helio I'd had on my ship, with my family, a front?

I stiffened as a hand came about my waist. "You ready to go?" Helio said gently.

"Yeah." I looked back at where the Osirian was still laying on the floor, surrounded by his brothers. "They're not coming?"

"They've chosen to stay back."

I couldn't say I was disappointed, but part of me did worry for the injured man and his brothers. No one should have to experience losing a sibling, and absolutely no one deserved to be there when it happened.

I wasn't the only one in the party that seemed somewhat relieved to be leaving the three men behind. As we turned away from them and left them with only one torch between the three, the Kushyami girl sighed deeply and spat backward towards them.

At first, I'd thought the troll was an unlucky and unlikely run-in, but the further we continued through the ruined city the more run-ins we had. Once we were able to get the trolls down, the Osirians killed them with their magic, but the smell of the blood lured out even more dangerous foes.

Wolvane usually hunted alone, would only track and kill lone travelers, and never lived in packs; so when we were attacked by a small pack of them it took us by surprise.

We heard creeping footsteps first. We simply thought they were other harmless creatures, but then came the rumble of growls. The Osirians summoned as much magic as they were willing to use as we drew our weapons once more and we fought, dodging teeth and claws the size of swords.

Each beast was as big as a troll but their movements were swifter. I wanted to thank Helio for insisting we bring that extra boat of Osirians because we'd be dead without them, but I realized that, too, only further proved my doubts were valid.

I tore my cutlass from the neck of the wolvane I had just killed, the blood splattering across my face, and turned to see where I was needed. Helio was holding his own quite well for someone who'd needed their grip corrected only a few hours ago. At least three Osirians were dead—including the woman I'd spoken to before, her head bitten clean off by one of the beasts—the rest were either faring all right, or at risk of joining the dead.

I leapt to the aid of a particularly small-framed Osirian pinned to the ground by a hulking wolvane paw. Jamming my blade into the creature's hind, I yanked it back out with just enough time to use it to hit away the beast's face before it could snap at mine. It tried to swat me down with its paw but I slashed at its fleshy underside. The wolvane, yelping in pain, danced back before lunging, its jaw extended.

I was ready.

I drove my cutlass through the roof of the wolvane's mouth and into its brain. Releasing the handle of my blade, I yanked my arm back from its mouth as the creature's eyes rolled back and it dropped to the floor, almost pulling me down with it. But I was not quick enough to avoid the sharp teeth raking my skin.

I hissed in pain as blood soaked the torn arm of my sleeve and kicked the beast's mouth open. Reaching in to retrieve my weapon, the handle now slick with saliva and blood, I had to brace my foot against the dead creature's upper jaw to muster enough force to free my blade. Once I had, I moved straight onto the next.

CHAPTER
23

After what felt like hours of relentless battle, the wolvane were finally dispatched. We lost six of our party to the beasts and now a majority were injured, the Osirians had exhausted their magic, and we were all too tired to keep moving. After stumbling upon a goblin residence that was just barely large enough to fit us all, we huddled inside together and lit a fire. Our supply of pickled vegetables and dried meat would not be enough for all of us, especially for us to eat enough to regain our energy to heal, so we cooked what was available—wolvane. I used what was left of the water in my flask to clean my wounds before healing them, knowing the wolvane saliva would only make them fester sooner.

"Here, let me," Helio said, coming to sit beside me after returning from moving the bodies of the dead away from where we were resting. He summoned his magic and I couldn't help but flinch away at first, the dark mist, in my mind, so deeply associated with times I wished I could forget. If Helio felt any emotion from my reaction he did not show it, he simply put all his energy into healing my arm.

"You fared quite well against that wolvane," I said, unable to get the vision of him fighting out of my mind.

"I guess that's all I needed for all my naval training to wake back up," he quipped.

"Just a wolvane pack attack?" I pressed, disbelief slipping into my tone.

He seemed to catch it because when Helio laughed it felt somewhat forced. "I guess so. It's been a long time, but I guess some things you never forget. It just takes a little extra danger to bring it to the surface."

After a short pause, I asked, "What do we do now?"

Helio's expression hardened. "We're not turning back."

"I agree, but I don't think the others will want to continue after this."

"Do you want to?" he asked, eyes locking onto mine, searching for an answer I wasn't sure I could give.

"I wasn't expecting so many to die," I whispered.

His eyes fell to the bone covered ground. "It has been more than expected. I knew there would be a risk and I should have shared that with you, I just thought you were all in."

My chest tightened at the thought of returning to Isidia empty-handed. This was meant to be my last hurrah, a chance to show Eevan and Islina that I could commit to something and follow through with it.

"And I am," I snipped, "I just don't think they are."

We both glanced around the small space at the remaining party. Many were nursing injuries, eating to regain their strength, or healing others—all looked drained.

"All we can do is ask, but they either stay and die, go back and possibly die, or come with us and possibly die." He shrugged. "The only difference is whether or not they want the glory."

"Or if they're greedy enough to follow us with hopes of taking it for themselves."

"You don't trust people easily, do you?"

"I've let you hang around, haven't I?"

"That doesn't mean you trust me," he said, his face angling up to meet mine.

"I suppose not," I murmured, catching a flicker of sadness pass over his features. "What's wrong?" I asked before I could stop myself, brushing the back of my hand along his cheek.

He sighed and leaned into my touch. "I just worry about how things will end." His hand stiffened above my arm, the wound still slowly knitting together. "We've been dancing around it, Bellona, but …" He paused, searching my face, his eyes glowing orange in the firelight from the torches lit within the house. "I truly care for you," he confessed. "Seeing you get so injured"—his gaze flickered to my arm—"I-I don't think I could take it again. If I hadn't been so exhausted already, I'd have killed every living thing in the cavern to keep you safe. I–This … it wasn't the plan." His eyes darted away from mine. "I was just meant to leave the tower, find the pieces, and claim the prize. This"—he motioned to the cave through the windows then back to me and waved his hand between us—"this wasn't the plan, and now I don't know what will happen. I don't like not knowing."

I stamped down all emotion, though everything within myself was screaming, my heart racing at his confession. "Sometimes we can't know how things will end."

"How do you want them to end?" he asked, his shoulders falling, as if he'd taken my words as a rejection. "How do you feel?"

"I will not answer that now," I said sternly. "As you've said, this was not the plan and I will not have emotions getting in the way. What we need to focus on right now is making it to the end of this journey, alive, and then we can address"— I motioned between us, as he had—"this."

He looked stunned and hurt for a moment, then seemed to sober before he nodded in agreement. "Of course." He rolled his shoulders and cracked his neck in an attempt to hide his dejection, but I could still see it. "Right—let's get this over with then."

Part of me wanted to soothe his mood and cast his doubts aside, but a stronger side of me insisted now was not the time. At that moment all that mattered was completing the journey. I could worry about this later—and I would.

Withdrawing his power, Helio said, "That's the best I can do. I'm sure your sister-in-law will be able to get rid of the scars."

I ran a hand up my arm, feeling the deep gouges running from mid-bicep to wrist—it was a miracle I hadn't died of blood loss. "Maybe I'll keep them," I mused.

Helio laughed. "Don't become a scar collector, they're so pathetic."

"I wouldn't say pathetic. Sentimental, maybe."

"I wouldn't have thought you to be particularly sentimental."

"I don't think many would," I said, unintentionally bitter.

Many people had it in their minds that I cared for nothing, that my recklessness was a sign of how little concern I had for myself, my life, and the people in it. But, if anything, it was my awareness of those things that fueled the recklessness. Elves lived long lives, but they could still come to an end at any moment. What purpose would be served in living a restricted life? In conforming to what was expected of a princess when there was so much more to be experienced and remembered? Too many Elves were in the habit of forgetting, living as long as we did, it was easy to. I liked remembering. Though I didn't keep large tokens, like Ikram, I had a small stash of keepsakes in my cabin, on my person, and back home. My ship itself was a keepsake—a gift from my brothers for surviving my first voyage—and on my ship were many reminders of my past. Past crew, past lovers, past battles. Triumphs and losses. All of it was marked and tallied within the wood of *The Siren*, there for me to remember for centuries to come.

"I didn't mean to insult you," Hello said softly.

"You didn't. I suppose I'm just tired of everyone assuming I care for nothing."

"They just don't realize that you have a different way of showing it."

"Blame it on their ignorance," I agreed and rested my head back on the wall behind us, closing my burning eyes. I was so tired. I longed to sleep but struggled without the light sway of the ocean, or the sound of waves lapping.

I had managed to drift off at some point, but it was a light sleep full of interruptions. With the snores of others, the loud drips, and occasional moans of the injured, it eventually reached a point where it seemed no one was able to sleep and we all gave up trying. I was about to stand and announce that Helio and I were continuing when he beat me to it, laying a hand on my shoulder, silently telling me to stay where I was.

"Captain Bellona and I are continuing through the caves," he said, loud enough for everyone to hear and turn their attention to him, but not loud enough for the sound to leak from the small house and into the overrun streets. "You are welcome to come with us if you can, or return to the ship."

I saw a few nod in agreement to join us, but also noticed many silently communicating with others, eyes widening, heads lightly shaking, eyebrows raising. I felt tension fill the air, and fear, and wondered to whom it was directed. It was the first time

Helio had addressed me as Captain, but not the first time I had sensed tension from others in his presence.

"We will be leaving soon. Take some time to consider your options," Helio said, and reached his hand down to help me up and lead us through the room full of scattered bodies and out the small door of the house.

"Quite the rousing speech," I quipped.

"I didn't think much more was needed."

We got the few that were carrying on with us together and left the rest in the house with those that were too wounded to carry on. We kept the torches low to the ground, hoping not to alert anymore wolvane to our presence—though the smell of blood would be enough to at least draw them close.

The further we ventured into the city, the more uneven the ground became, the crystallized skeletons of long-dead goblins piling higher and higher. The poor bastards had been cornered, they had nowhere to run but deeper into the caves, and I was sure the piles would only get higher as we continued on.

The group kept quiet as we traveled, all of us terrified of what other creatures could be lurking in the depths of the city. Every now and then someone would give a gasp of shock as their foot sank through the base of a skull, or they nipped an ankle on a sharp piece of crystal. Each time that happened we would all pause for a moment and listen. But the surrounding caves had gone silent, aside from our crunching and the never-ending drips. It was an uncomfortable level of silence. The kind of silence that meant something was waiting for us at the end of the road. And after hours of walking, we learned what that thing was.

At first, it stood still, and I thought it nothing but another carving on the wall— goblins did love their carvings. The style matched those of the Shinchaku temple, as if they'd all been crafted by the same hand. As I looked closer, the silhouette took shape; it was troll-like in appearance, except its arms were ever-so-slightly shorter, so they didn't drag on the ground. It stood before a steep staircase that led to a lower level. After a moment of pause before the statue, I moved to continue past it, but Helio quickly moved to grab my hand and pull me back.

CHAPTER 24

"Everyone stop!" Helio warned, "That's not just a harmless statue."

"What is it?" the Kushyami girl asked.

"Something that could kill us all. It's enchanted—old goblin magic. When you get close to it, it will come alive and do everything it can to stop you getting past it."

"There's no way to stop it?" I asked.

Helio paused in thought for a moment before he pulled his tattered notebook from his satchel and flicked through the pages. "There may be one way, but I can't be sure it'll work," he murmured, still reading from his notes. "There should be a special object, a gem or precious metal, somewhere on the creature's body that's its power source. The guardian statues are too big—*were* too big—for goblins to enchant themselves, so they would use metals and gems to amplify their power and embed them into the stones."

"So we just have to locate and remove the enchanted stone?" I asked, and Helio nodded in confirmation. "How close do we need to be to activate it?"

"Each one is different," he said in an apologetic tone.

I sighed, pinching the bridge of my nose, and closed my eyes for a moment to think. "Let's see if we can find the object without activating the guardian. If it does activate—"

"You and Helio should continue. We will stay back and fight the creature," a lanky Osirian declared.

It took me a moment to properly mask my surprise. "You all agree to this?" I asked.

There was a silent pause, the remainder of the crewmates shared glances between themselves before they all nodded in agreement. Only the Kushyami girl hesitated, her eyes flicking between Helio and I. I thought I caught a glimpse of warning in her eyes before she quickly turned away and joined the rest in trying to find the hidden object.

We stood shoulder to shoulder before the guardian, each of us waiting for another to start looking first.

"It's probably on its back," I muttered.

"Well, you're more than welcome to take a look," an Osirian next to me replied.

I sighed and stepped back from the group, pacing behind them and studying the guardian as much as I could from a distance. All I could see was roughly carved stone; there were no runes, no other markings, no glittering jewels or metals. I turned away from the group to stare into the darkness behind us, clearing my mind and vision of all distractions. If the jewel was on the back, our only option was to set it off and hope for the best—the same would be the case if it were under the arms or by the leg joins, both difficult areas to get to when the creature was stationary. Setting it off was our only option.

I'd never fought a living stone before. It should have filled me with dread but, instead, excitement sparked through me. I tried to think of a plan, a way to arrange us that could minimize casualties. Had it been my crew with me, I could have had a plan in seconds, but I knew nothing of the people I was with. I didn't know their strengths or weaknesses, if they favored fighting low or high, relied on speed over strength.

A cry echoed through the cavern followed by the scraping of boots on stone from behind me. I spun to see the Kushyami girl, eyes wide, staring at me from the ground before the guardian, everyone else had stepped back and reached desperately for their weapons.

"Bell—" she started, but the rest of my name and whatever else she'd wanted to say never passed her lips. I'd barely had time to blink and register what had happened before the girl's small form was crushed by the end of a large stone arm. I stared at the ground where she had previously stood. Her locs flared around the edges of the guardian's arm, soaking in the blood and splinters of bone surrounding the mass of stone. My stomach turned at the sight, but I pushed the nausea down. I'd seen the same and worse in the war, and now was no time to be shocked by it.

The creature moved faster than I ever could have anticipated. In two short breaths, it had lifted its arm from the ruin of the Kushyami girl and taken down two more of the party, spraying their blood across us all as it swung its arms at its next target.

"Helio!" Exclaimed the lanky Osirian. "Bellona! Go!" He directed as he leaped out of the way of the guardian's arms.

Helio seemed to materialize out of the darkness beside me and gripped my elbow, dragging me toward the now unguarded staircase. "Wait!" I called. "We can't leave them."

"They'll be fine!" He argued.

I fought out of his grip and spun to face the battle. The Osirians were doing their best to dodge the guardian's attacks but had still lost one more in the short time I'd been looking away. Apart from the ominous grinding of the stone, the creature made no other noise—it did not breathe or roar. I scanned the back of the creature, as thoroughly and quickly as possible. If I had to leave them, I at least wanted to leave them knowing that I had given them a chance at survival. The back of the guardian was almost completely smooth. A few knicks or scratches could be seen on its surface, but as it stepped slightly sideways and caught the torchlight at a different angle, I spotted a slight glimmer by its right knee joint. It wasn't the glimmer of precious gems or jewels, it was metal. Iron, I guessed, based on the pattern of rust.

"Its right knee!" I called back to the party. "The metal is in the knee joint!"

The few who weren't actively fighting for their lives acknowledged my words and set to work trying to hit the target. Helio once again grabbed my arm and tried pulling me away from the fight, but I refused to move until I felt that they had some kind of chance. They managed to form a circle around it, one side tried to draw the creature's attention so the other could attack the knee, but it moved so quickly it was almost impossible to land a hit. Every time someone got close it spun to attack them and so on.

"Bell," Helio pleaded, "we need to go now—before it spots us. They'll be fine," he assured me.

With one last look at the fighting Osirians, I let Helio grab hold of my hand and pull me down the steep stairs into the depths of the cave.

The air grew more and more moist as we went until it was almost too thick to breathe normally. Even Helio began to struggle and requested frequent breaks, but I couldn't rest, I could barely sit still. My mind kept wandering back up the stairs and to the battle with the guardian. Had they all been killed? Had they defeated the creature? And, more importantly, what awaited us at the base of these stairs?

CHAPTER 25

Helio took deep, steadying breaths as we made our way down the last lot of stairs. It felt as if we'd been walking down them for days, but I knew it was the illusion of darkness that made it feel that way. It had more than likely only taken us a few long hours. We were unsteady on our legs, even more so than a sailor stepping on land for the first time in years. Once we reached the base we collapsed to the ground and couldn't stand.

"I guess we're being forced to rest." Helio chuckled as he tried and failed to raise to his knees.

I dumped my pack on the stair behind me and lay back on it, staring up at the darkness above, trying to keep my mind from wondering what could be hiding in it.

"Thank fuck," I murmured and closed my eyes. "Do you think we're close?" I asked after a moment's silence.

I heard Helio shift to lay down beside me. "I hope so." He sighed. "I don't know how much more of this cave I can take."

"I figured you'd be used to it, assuming you spend all day and night in the library."

"Yes, but the library has windows and is above ground."

I grunted in response, exhaustion finally catching up with me, and I couldn't bring myself to speak.

Helio curled up to my side and, despite the humidity, wrapped my arm around his neck and rested his head on my shoulder. "Sleep well, Bellona," he whispered in my ear.

I grunted again and fell into my dreams.

I woke on my side, my body curled around Helio's, the arm tucked under his head completely numb, and my stomach rumbling with hunger. Opening my eyes, I flinched at the light, and wiggled my fingers to get the feeling back, waking

Helio as the muscles flexed beneath his head. I let Helio's head drop onto his hard pack as I sat up quickly, causing him to grumble. But I ignored him as I stared up at the ceiling above us. It was blue, but too bright to be the morning sky and I could see smooth ripples winding their way through it, like blue flames licking their way across a wooden ceiling.

"A glacier," Helio said. "We must have walked through to the other side of the island and under the glaciers."

"Well, the dampness makes sense now."

"At least we can see without lighting a torch—my arm aches from holding that thing."

I rolled my eyes, but I too was glad for the natural light. It relieved the feeling of being trapped below ground just enough that a small amount of the panic inside me ebbed away. I dug through our packs for food and found a small amount of dried meat, as tough as boot leather, and wished I'd had the sense to refill our packs with wolvane meat before leaving the others.

"Let's hope we're close to being done. We don't have a lot of food left," I said as I tossed a strip to Helio.

I gazed around the dimly lit space as I ate. It was just as large as the previous area, if not larger. The ice ceiling cast the cavern in a thin blue light that made the stalagmites glitter; to the right of the stairs and the ledge we were on was a sheer drop into darkness. I was thankful that Helio and I had just passed out the night before and not tried to explore the area first, because the chances of us not walking off the edge would have been very slim. I turned to look in the direction opposite the stairs, the way we would be traveling, the only way we could go, and my mouth went dry.

"Not this shit again!" I exclaimed. Large pits broke up the rest of the path before us, narrow strips of earth between them—and no way around in sight. They'd been hidden from view while we'd been sitting, but had appeared like a slap in the face as soon as we stood. Immediately, I slumped to the ground and began stretching out my still-sore legs.

"This treasure better be fucking worth it," I mumbled.

"If we weren't so close, I would give up right now," Helio whined as he joined me in stretching.

We were both wincing and limping as we rose back to our feet and approached the first pit. The distance to the other side wasn't too far, but I knew it would be the same as the temple in Shinchaku, that the distance between the pits would grow as we went on. I just hoped we had enough energy to get us over them.

We easily jumped the first three, but began to struggle after the fourth. Helio was finding it increasingly difficult to breathe in the thick, moist air and our legs were nowhere close to having recovered after the stairs. Each time we landed after a jump, we'd struggle to get upright as our legs desperately wanted to collapse under our weight.

But I could see the end ahead. I took some deep, gulping breaths and charged forward, leaping once, running, leaping twice, running, and leaping a third time over the last pit. I staggered forward before my legs gave way and I fell to my knees, breathing heavily through the pain spiking through them.

"You made that look so easy." Helio huffed.

I turned to face him, still on my knees, and watched as he gave a few bounces before sucking in air and doing the same thing I did, only he was coming up too short on the early jumps.

"Helio." I tried to warn him, but he didn't seem to hear. On the second last jump, he cleared the pit by a hair. "Helio," I said again, "Helio, wait!" But I was too late.

He jumped too soon—the toes of his front foot barely scraped the edge of the pit.

I rushed to my feet as our eyes locked and I registered his fear. He was already slipping out of sight beneath the ledge of the pit as I dove, sliding along the ground. My skin scraped along the stone and I hissed, arms outstretched, catching his arms just before he fell out of reach. The force of him falling pulled me right to the edge until the jagged rock dug painfully into my armpits, and Helio's weight threatened to pull my arms from their sockets. I cried out in pain, the sound scraping my throat as it was forced out, when my fingers—wrapped tightly around Helio's forearms—were slammed against the rock face. For a moment all we could do was stare at each other and breathe, our minds still lagging seconds behind our physical reactions.

Then the panic set in.

Helio's eyes widened further. His breathing came short and fast, his grip on my forearms tightening to the point of pain. "I'm sorry," he rambled, "I should have stopped. But if I'd stopped I wouldn't have been able to continue."

"Shh," I soothed with a grunt as I tried to pull him up, gritting my teeth against the painful strain of my muscles.

Helio's eyes welled with tears as my shoulders collapsed under the weight of him. He took a few deep breaths, closing his eyes and resting his head against his outstretched arm. "Bell," he whispered, "Bell, just let me go."

I shook my head. "No!" I said through gritted teeth, "I can pull you up. We're getting through this." I attempted to pull him up again, groaning with effort as I tried to use the strength in my arms alone to lift, my cry echoing through the cavern.

"Bellona!" Helio yelled, my name bouncing around the cave until it sounded as if a chorus of people were yelling at me. "Let–let go. I made it this far, that's enough for me."

Tears sprung to my own eyes as the realization of what letting go would mean finally hit me. "No." I gasped. "I can't let go." I grunted with effort as I pulled once again. "I'm not letting you go!" I yelled as I used every bit of strength left in me, every muscle available, to pull Helio up. My whole body tensed, my back burned, my shoulders ached as I hauled Helio up. My stomach and legs strained as I moved, still hauling Helio, from my stomach, to my knees, to sitting, pulling him on top of me with the same motion I'd use for rowing a boat.

It took a moment for us to comprehend what had just happened, that he was now safe. We lay, Helio on top of me, staring at each other, our faces close enough that we shared each other's breath, for the gods only know how long. Until Helio began to laugh and I followed until our laughter, turned into sobbing.

"I thought that was the end," Helio breathed, his head falling to rest on my chest. "I was so sure I would die."

"I wouldn't let you die," I said before I could stop myself. I brought a hand up to run it through his white hair as he wept into my chest.

"I didn't want that to be my last image of you," he said.

"It won't be," I whispered.

I held him until he calmed, then we decided that was enough excitement for one day and set up to sleep. We couldn't stomach food, so we just set our packs on the floor and slept, holding on to each other as tightly as we could.

CHAPTER
26

The tall, stone double door stood before us. We didn't know what to expect on the other side, but I had a feeling it wouldn't be anything pleasant—nothing in this cavern had been.

We'd woken before the sun had risen, but waited till it had to move, not trusting that we'd be safe from accidentally getting too close to the cliff face. Once the cavern was again full of blue light shining through the glacier ceiling, we rose and packed up our bags. Our movements were slow, most followed by winces.

The door before us was only slightly smaller than the first we'd encountered. A cold wind seemed to seep through its cracks, and even brighter blue light flooded from beneath it. We held our breath as we pushed them open, eager to see what lay on the other side, to finally lay eyes on what the treasure truly was. The doors groaned open slowly, and I found myself wincing as pain laced its way up my back and through my shoulders. Before we did anything else, I needed Helio to heal me, but before I could make the request, we both groaned as our eyes fell on what awaited us through the threshold.

There didn't seem to be any traps lying in wait, nor any guardians, just a large pool of crystal-clear water, a thin layer of mist drifting above it. I stepped through the door and gazed down into what I'd thought was a pool, only to discover it was a flooded subterranean crypt. The ceiling in the new room was also completely made up of ice. From my very limited view of the pool from the doorway, I could see that this extended down through the water, illuminating the whole other lower level.

The goblins had carved their way through the underside of the island—through the belly of a glacier—only to leave their dead in the most beautiful part of the whole underground world they'd created.

"I'm guessing whatever we're looking for is down there," I said, gesturing toward the pool.

Helio nodded, his lips pursed. He just stood and stared down at the pool, frozen. I waited to see if he would say anything more, but he remained silent.

I sighed and began to disrobe, but paused as I noticed Helio snapping out of his trance and following my lead. "What are you doing?"

"I didn't pack extra clothes and I'd rather not freeze to death in these ones."

"You're Osirian, you won't freeze," I said, unable to stop myself from rolling my eyes at him, "and who said you were coming with me?" I figured this was the reason I was here. "That pool could be thousands of fathoms deep—there's no way you'd survive."

"There'll be air pockets," he said, waving at me dismissively. "I was in the navy, I'm a good swimmer."

"Fine. If you drown I'm leaving your body down there."

"Sure you will," he whispered into my ear as he stepped past me into the pool, wearing only his braies.

I pulled on my stiff swimming clothes. The waxed fabric wouldn't keep me completely dry, but it would slow how quickly I'd feel the cold and offer some small amount of protection from any dangers that may be lurking beneath the surface of the water. I quickly tied off the limb openings until they were uncomfortably tight against my upper arms, legs, and neck, then joined Helio in the water.

I tensed as I took the first step in, expecting the water to be icy, but found it to be surprisingly pleasant.

"Underwater volcanoes—they're all over the place around here," Helio said, grinning at my confusion.

"I know about underwater volcanoes. I just wasn't expecting warm water inside a glacier," I snapped, stepping further into the tepid water. "You ready?" I asked, flicking my eyes to a submerged staircase.

Helio nodded and sucked in a breath, his chest and stomach expanding out as he filled his lungs with as much air as possible before he dove under the surface. I did the same, even though I didn't require the air. It was better to have it than have nothing.

I dove beneath the surface of the clear water and followed Helio as he swam down toward the depths of the tomb. I held my mouth slightly open to let the water pass through, the feel of it flowing back out through my gills almost causing me to shiver.

The Isidians had once tried to explain to me how my gills worked, how exactly my body managed to pull the air from the water and make it possible for me to not need my lungs. But I had retained none of it. As long as they worked, I didn't care how.

The feeling of being underwater again, for me, was as if I'd smoked the strongest and most pleasant drug. My head felt clear, my limbs steady, and for once I wasn't drenched in sweat. Helio had done the best an Osirian could to heal my muscles, but they'd still ached a little. Now, under the water, I could barely tell. Being weightless took all of my pain away, pain I hadn't even realized I had until it was gone. Every now and then I had to stop the flow of water into my mouth;

otherwise, I would get too much air, and my head would become light, my vision blurry. "Too much of a good thing" also applied to things we needed to live.

The stone walls that closed in around us beneath the surface were covered in burial memorials, whole sections dedicated to a singular clan; other areas, more empty than the rest, appeared to be saved for only the gods knew who. At first I'd thought I'd have to push Helio away from studying the sites, but he swam past them with barely a single glance at the runes. It seemed, when he wanted to, he could exhibit self-control.

The glacier sloped down naturally and the floor of the goblin structure followed. We dove, continuing through the passage. Helio had held his breath longer than I thought possible for a regular elf, and just when I was starting to grow concerned, he arched upward in the water and kicked furiously toward a silvery, rippling air pocket. I swam up to join him, our bodies pressed together beneath the water as our heads rose into the pocket.

"You doing alright?" I asked as Helio gasped for air.

"I'm doing the best I can," Helio gasped out. "I hate that you're not struggling in the slightest."

I winked and slid back under the water, allowing him to catch his breath in private. The water had been growing warmer the further down we swam, I could only hope that it wouldn't get to unbearable levels, which most likely meant we were getting closer to the bottom. Helio joined me back under the water after a few long minutes and we proceeded down, the walls of tombs continuing down with us until we reached a flat rock face with an archway carved through the middle.

This is it! I mouthed to Helio.

He nodded, wide-eyed.

We dipped below the top of the arch and swam through.

Tombs no longer lined the walls, in their stead stood statues, large and small, of sea creatures and goblins alike. I'd never thought of goblins as having any kind of reverence for the sea or its creatures, but from the few ruins I'd now seen, I realized how little I really knew about the goblins. It made sense the more I thought about it. They would be sibling creations of the gods, perhaps the sea creatures even came first—I really didn't know. Peverell would've known. He would have taken the time to pull me aside and explain everything we'd seen in this cavern. I would have acted as if I were ignoring him, but kept the knowledge stored away in my mind for a day when I could use it against him.

A sharp pain lanced through my right arm, reminding me to keep my mind on the task at hand. I pulled to the side and floated in place, glancing around to see what had injured me. To my right, a jet of bubbling hot water was shooting up from the floor of the flooded room. The glacier cooled the majority of the water down to a pleasant enough temperature, but the jets themselves were scalding hot.

Helio swam up to me to inspect the arm I'd burnt. I pulled it from his grasp and mouthed, *I'm fine.*

He squinted at me in disbelief and I rolled my eyes in response, then I noticed his eyes flick up and quickly around, panic rising in them. I gripped his shoulders to get his attention, questioning him with my eyes. He raised his hands to his throat, as he had in Shinchaku. Air. He needed air.

He wouldn't make it to the nearest air pocket in the other section of the pool, and the current room had none. I locked my mouth over his and slowly emptied the air held in my lungs into his. Between two normal beings, this would not work, but my own abnormality made it possible. When my gills were doing the breathing, my lungs became nothing but air storage sacks.

Helio's hands clamped to the sides of my face as he accepted the air. Once my lungs were emptied, I motioned for him to swim back to the last air pocket. He shook his head and jabbed his finger down toward the ground. I shook my head in return and began to push him back toward the archway. Helio fought against me for a moment before locking eyes with me, and whatever he saw in mine made him stop his struggling. With a final pat on my cheek, he desperately swam back to the air pocket. I hoped he would see sense and swim all the way back to the surface, but I knew he wouldn't, I could only pray that he wouldn't get too tired to keep himself above water.

I dove, swimming at a faster speed than I could when Helio was with me, steering clear of the scalding jets of volcanically heated water. At the lower level, I could see how the sea life had begun to creep in and consume the ruins. Crustaceans of all kinds scuttled along the ground, snapping at any of the tiny fish that swam too close and picking at the strange algae that grew around the vents. Coral had begun to spread its way along the floor and walls of the last chamber, barely leaving any evidence of the goblin civilization.

I realized, as I got close to them, that what I had first thought were statues of goblins were actually goblin remains, weighed down in the depths by their heavy metal armor. I'd swum through many an underwater graveyard, but none so eerie as this flooded, literal graveyard. Despite the light shining through the glacier ceiling, the water seemed to grow darker as I swam. My head began to feel light, as if I'd held my breath for too long, but I wasn't holding my breath at all. I felt my neck, to be sure there was nothing blocking my gills and the flow of water through them. There was no obstacle. I did my best to ignore the feeling. I concluded it must've been the vents. Volcanoes above the sea filled the air with poison; I wouldn't be surprised if they did the same below water, but I'd never been close enough to experience it.

I kicked with all my might to continue through the water. I could see the end—it was just up ahead. A throne, large to a goblin but small to an elf, sat against the back wall, covered in the same carvings as every other goblin ruin I'd seen. Runes I couldn't read wrapped around the arms and top of the stone chair and sat in its seat were the remains of a goblin ruler, held down in place by a chest plate. The skeleton was in pristine condition. I was surprised the bone-eating worms of the sea hadn't gotten to it yet. The clothes they'd worn in their last moments hung from their bones, drifting in the light current. Despite their being dead, their head was held high, resting against the back of the throne, as if even in death they held watch over their people. I wondered if Darius would be that dedicated of a ruler.

I studied the body, looking for anything that seemed important enough to warrant the journey we'd been on. The crown that rested on the goblin's skull didn't look to be anything special, just a heavy piece of unexciting metal. But maybe that was it? Did I know what I was looking for? The water seemed to ripple in an impossible pattern, and pain shot through my skull. I needed to find whatever I was looking for. Quickly.

When I moved my hands again, there seemed to be five of them, all reaching forward to shift the skeleton. My vision blurred and as it did, something glinted in a way that seemed to call to me. I tried to stop my movements so the water wouldn't shift the item out of glinting range, but it already had. I wanted to sigh but there was no air in my lungs to do so. Reaching forward once more, all I could do was hope the movement in the water was what was triggering the glinting. What had Peverell said to look for? Pain lanced through my head again just as the glint reappeared in my blurry field of view—I snatched for it.

My hands closed over something, but it was attached to something else. I tried to pull it but it wouldn't come loose. I closed my eyes for a moment and reopened them to clear my vision. It worked for a quick second, enough time for me to see that it was attached to the arm of the dead goblin ruler.

Bracelet! My mind screamed at me. Peverell had said it would be a bracelet. I held the edge of the tiny metal hoop in one hand and snapped the wrist of the goblin ruler with the other, freeing the bracelet.

I pushed off the ground and shot up through the water, my head still pounding, vision blurry, and just hoped the bracelet was the right artifact because there was no way I was going back down near the vents. Shooting up through the water forced more bad water through my gills before I got to the good stuff. Things got worse before they got better. It was the closest I'd ever come to drowning. My head pounded so hard, all I wanted to do was rip my eyes from their sockets in the hopes it would relieve some pressure.

And then, almost as quickly as it had come on, it stopped.

The pain dissipated, my vision cleared with a blink, and my mind settled. The water was finally cooler and cleaner, and I could breathe again. I took a moment to pause, suspended in the water, to study the bracelet. It was a tiny thing, forged for tiny goblin wrists. Silver with a blue gem in the center, it seemed to hum with an energy I hadn't noticed before. I wished I had more time to examine it alone, but I longed to get out of the water—and out of the ruins altogether.

Helio was still floating with his head in the air-pocket when I reached him and tugged on his leg to let him know I had returned. I trusted that he could manage his own way back and swam ahead. I just wanted a moment out of the water to study the bracelet myself.

CHAPTER 27

I wasted no time as I reached the water's edge. Stalking out of the pool, bracelet in hand, I sat on the solid ground and held it up to the light to check for any engravings, but saw none. It really was just a simple bangle with a gem in it. But I could sense the power in it, a hum of restless energy that felt very familiar.

"Let me see it," Helio demanded. I hadn't even heard him surface from the pool. He crouched down before me, his white hair hanging wet and limp around his face. A wave of anger rolled over me at his tone, but he had been like this concerning the treasure for the whole last leg of the journey.

I held the bracelet out to him, schooling my features into a disinterested expression.

"Not that," he said, pushing it away and reaching for my burnt arm. "Didn't I ask you not to get hurt again?" he chided, yanking me forward so he could get a better look at my arm.

"It's not like I planned to get burned," I snapped back, hiding my surprise at his concern.

He raised his hand to heal me, the black mist drowning out the light around us. I'd barely remembered that the burn was there and, looking down, could see that it was barely worth worrying about.

"Right, now that that's done," he said, patting my now healed arm, "let's look at this treasure." I dropped the bracelet into his open palm and watched him as he brought it up to his eyes and studied it. "Bit plain, isn't it? I've got hundreds just like it," he said, picking up the bracelet between forefinger and thumb and turning it this way and that. Finally, he sighed and handed it back to me. "I hope it was worth all this."

"I suppose we'll find out the hard way," I said, placing the bracelet safely into my bag. I then lay down, completely exhausted, on the shore of the pool, the water lapping lazily at my feet.

Helio spread out beside me and not long after his breathing slowed to that of sleep. I rolled onto my side to look at him. His hair had fallen away from his face, the blue glow from the glacier above us turning his skin a more common shade of purple for an Osirian. He had seemed so disinterested in the bracelet, and yet this pool seemed to be the only thing that would have warranted his need for me. He must have known about it somehow, but I couldn't be sure if it was because he'd studied and read about it ... or because he'd been here and failed before. But, surely, if he'd been to the cavern before he'd have been more prepared for the trials we'd faced? We'd lost so many in the battles with the wolvane and the guardian, and Helio did not strike me as the kind of person to waste a life so easily.

The fearful Minoman man flickered into my mind.

Helio had not thought twice about sending him to his death—and had certainly not felt remorse for it. It could have been because he'd wanted to solidify his position of power over the hired crew, but it hadn't felt necessary at the time. The thoughts left me questioning who was being lied to. The hired crew, me, or was Helio lying to himself?

As it was in the Shinchaku temple, the journey back was much easier, and in no time we were making our way cautiously up the stairs where we'd left the remaining crew to fight the guardian.

The cavern above was silent. I prayed that it was because the crew had been victorious in defeating the guardian and not because they were all splayed out on the cave floor, crushed by the stone arms of the goblin creation.

We grew more cautious the closer we got to the top of the stairs, doing our best to make as little noise as possible. I held my breath as the last step came into view and didn't release it until I saw nothing but empty space at the top.

The guardian was nowhere to be seen.

Helio and I sighed with relief as we climbed the last couple of steps. There was a pile of bodies, haphazardly stacked by the entrance to the staircase, and before them lay a pile of crumbled stone.

"They did it." I marveled aloud.

"I won't lie, I expected to have to fight our way out," Helio said, kicking at one of the loose stones with his booted foot.

"There's still the wolvane, and with less of us we're ripe for the picking," I reminded him grimly.

"It does make it easier for us to sneak through, though."

With that, we continued our journey back through the cavern, only stopping for one short sleep on the way. We met no live wolvane on the trek back through, but did encounter many more dead ones and a couple more lost crew members. By my count, there would only be a few left—if any at all.

I felt more and more relieved as we got closer to the mouth of the cave, but also more exposed, the bright light leaving us visible and open for an easy attack. I was unsure where my unease was coming from. Perhaps the journey out had felt too easy and the imbalance caused my mind to fret over the small things. There would be no one else on this deserted island except the people we'd paid to be there, so there shouldn't have been anything to fear.

I didn't feel any more or less relief after we met with the remaining crew. The two large Osirians had clearly lost their brother and sat away from the others, silently grieving. The other Osirians stood to welcome us back. Most ignored me, but they all took the chance to clap Helio on the shoulder. None asked us whether or not we'd been successful, they simply packed up the small camp they'd set and we continued our trek down to the beach and waiting boats—all of us eager to return to the ship and, hopefully, our normal lives.

We returned to the ship in our empty boats after nightfall. We'd run out of oil and flint and were left to row in the dark, with only the dim moonlight to guide us through the water. I found myself staring down into the black depths rather than into the glowing yellow eyes of my comrades. I found everyone beautiful and was very rarely put off by appearances, but Osirians in the darkness of night bore a closer resemblance to pit beasts than elves. The color was leached from their skin by the darkness, yet their eyes and hair seemed to catch and hold whatever light there was. In another time and place, I could imagine it being quite alluring … but over the open ocean it was a thing of nightmares.

"You survived," Captain Adra said by way of greeting as we climbed aboard, "and lost half my crew."

"Barely half," Helio snipped back. "There's enough to get us home."

"And where is home?" the captain asked.

"Kushyam," Helio said without so much as a glance at me.

"Then I guess we're going to Kushyam," the Captain said and began barking orders at her crew.

Helio grasped my hand and led me down to our cabin, closing the door and locking it behind us. I threw my bag down and collapsed onto the cot with a sigh.

"I never want to get out of bed again." Every muscle in my body seemed to liquify and sink into the mattress—the thought of moving caused physical pain.

Helio laughed. "Good. I don't want you to leave the bed for the remainder of the trip," he said with a sly grin. "I want to enjoy every minute of however long I have left with you," he whispered as he knelt beside me on the bed, running a hand up my leg.

"You say that like you expect it to end," I whispered back.

"I have hope that it won't," he replied, now tracing the lines of muscle in my bare arms. "But with you, it's hard to know where I stand."

"Why do you need to know?" I asked, resisting the urge to shiver under his touch. "Can't we just enjoy the moment and see where it takes us?"

"I wish it were that simple," he said into my ear.

"Then make it simple."

He pulled back and met my eyes as his hand came to rest lightly on my waist. "Bellona," he said, then paused.

My breath caught.

"Bellona," he repeated, breathlessly, "I don't want this to end when we return to Kushyam. I don't want this to be a quick relationship, I want this to last." He reached for my hand and laced our fingers together, bringing them to rest against his chest so that I could feel his heart pounding away beneath them. "Bell, I ... I—"

I pressed my free hand gently against his lips, stopping him from saying what I wasn't ready to hear.

"I'm not ready for this to end either," I said quickly, before he thought otherwise. "But I'm not ready for ... *that*." His eyes softened slightly at my words. "Not yet," I whispered.

He smiled and nodded, gently removing my hand from his mouth and leaning down to kiss me. My arms wrapped around his neck and pulled him on top of me. Before long, our clothes were discarded and we were absorbed with each other. We were gentle, passionate and slow—in some ways the opposite of what had become our normal—but this time meant more, it meant something. Every other time we'd been together paled in comparison to this. When it was over we clung to each other, despite the uncomfortable humidity of the room, and that's what it was like for days after we left the island. We were always together, always in the cabin, using our bodies to express the feelings that couldn't be said, only leaving when we couldn't avoid it.

One night I lay on the bed, fiddling with the bracelet as Helio sat on the floor, my brother's notes and his own scattered around him.

"How much more could there be to translate?" I asked, only half interested in an answer.

"You'd be surprised," Helio said. "We vaguely know what the bracelet does, but I want to know the extent of it. How much magic can it ward against and how could we use it today?"

"Do we need to worry about warding against fairy magic these days?" I asked, even more disinterested.

"You never know. They've been confined to that forest for so long, maybe they'll try breaking out."

"Now, wouldn't that be interesting?" I mused, thinking of the chaos that would ensue.

"I wish it were as simple as taking it apart and putting it back together again," Helio said as he scribbled something out in his notes. "Trying to decipher ancient text and magic is so tedious."

The ship suddenly lurched to a halt. Helio's papers slid away from him along the floor. I just managed to close my hand around the bracelet before I could drop it as I rolled off the bed and onto the floor with a thud.

"What the fuck?"

"We're nowhere near the border, we shouldn't have been stopped yet." Helio said, rising quickly to his feet. "Wait down here," he told me, "I'll see what's going on. Do not come upstairs in case it is a patrol."

I waved a dismissive hand.

"Bellona," he said sternly, "I'm serious."

"Alright. I'll stay here until you come back."

He nodded and left the room, quietly shutting the door behind him.

At first, everything seemed normal. The same amount of noise echoed down the hallway from the upper deck, the same number of footsteps thumped overhead. But then there came more, more than I'd ever heard on the ship, and the ringing of clashing blades.

Panic filled me. Was it the Osirians? The Shinchaku? Or pirates? Who else knew about the bracelet and our journey? It couldn't be Peverell. Jarrel would never attack a ship without my orders. And they wouldn't have known I was on this ship. I hadn't been above deck all day.

It was torture listening to the cries and clangs of battle and not being able to join. Even more so when I couldn't be sure who was winning and I had nowhere else to go if my side lost. I stood at the door, my hand on the handle, sword drawn and ear pressed to the wood, listening for approaching footsteps. None ventured below deck as the battle rocked the ship.

It must have been a whole hour—or two, or three—before the commotion quietened. And, for all of it, I held my position. But once it grew silent, and it didn't sound as if anyone were coming for me, I opened the door and crept out into the hallway, sword raised. No one had come down to the lower deck, but I could hear voices trailing down the stairs.

Cautiously, I approached, being careful not to make any noise as I slowly climbed them. I was halfway up when I heard Helio's voice. Relief flooded me, first because he was alive and second because it sounded as if he had the upper hand. Behind his voice was a myriad of noises I couldn't quite make out, and I decided to stay quiet and observe, rather than face his anger at me putting myself in possible danger again.

After making sure I was clear, I poked my head above the edge of the main deck from the stairwell and was finally able to see what had happened.

My breath caught. Off the port side of the ship was another vessel, covered in roaring flames, the mast crackling under the heat of the blaze. On the deck, a handful of naval officers knelt before Helio and the crew of *The Maiden*. Captain Adra stood closely behind Helio. She was almost unrecognizable, a cruel grin spread across her face as she stared down at the officers with their hands tied behind their backs.

"I take it this wasn't how you expected things to go when you performed an illegal raid today, Weth," Helio said, addressing the Captain knelt before him.

"I certainly didn't expect to see you," The Captain shot back, her voice low and rasping in a way that made me think she'd once had her throat slit. "I must confess, I was disappointed when rumors spread that you'd been killed." Helio's brows furrowed at her words. "Only because I wanted that pleasure myself." Weth spat on the deck by Helio's boots.

Helio laughed ... only, it didn't sound like a laugh I'd heard from him before. It was sharp and cruel sounding. "Yet here we are, with you at my feet"—he stepped forward, grabbing the Captain's chin roughly and forcing her to look at him—"waiting to die." He sneered.

The feral cruelty in his voice sent a cold sweat down my spine. I sucked in a breath and tightened my grip on my sword. *Listen to the rest*, I told myself, *he could still be in the right.*

"How shall I do it?" he asked, addressing the crew behind him, tossing the Captain's face away and rising to face the crowd, they jeered. "Quick, painless, merciful?" He turned back to Weth, leaning down until his eyes were level with hers. "Or slow, painful, torturous?"

The crowd cheered, but Helio didn't react. His eyes were locked with Weth's, pure rage written all over his features. "Sounds like my crew's made the decision for me."

His crew? The words slapped me. *His crew*, my mind repeated.

"And what of my crew? Those that remain, what will you do to them?" Weth asked, her voice unwavering.

Without blinking, Helio summoned his power and killed all the remaining crew in the span of a single heartbeat. My stomach fell, my chest tightening. I could hardly breathe as I watched the cloud of black mist dissipate into the air and the bodies thud down onto the deck. There had to have been twenty, if not thirty, people there.

With the snap of a finger, Helio had killed them all.

"Shall we begin? I have someone waiting for me," he said smugly.

I was that someone.

My mind raced in time with my heartbeat, breath coming short and fast. I almost dropped my sword and gave away my position as a keening scream sounded across the deck. I had to get out of there, but how? The only way was to cross the deck. Unless there were windows somewhere below.

My legs didn't want to move, so I practically slid back down the stairs and somehow made it back to my cabin. Changing into my swimming clothes, I retrieved what was important— tucking as much of the paper and delicate items inside it as I could—and just hoped they would survive the swim. I wanted Peverell to get his research back. He deserved that much, especially when he'd been right all along.

I bit my lip to distract from the tears that threatened to flow. After everything we'd been through, he'd still lied to me. I'd suspected, of course, I wasn't fucking stupid, but this was a level of betrayal I hadn't imagined. A hidden identity, sure, but to have a whole crew, manipulate me into caring, into … I drove my fist into the wall, the skin across my knuckles splitting, blood running down my fingers.

Shaking so hard with rage that I could barely see straight, I kicked off my boots—I couldn't wear them to swim anyway—and entered the hallway again. It was only in the hallway that I could hear what was going on above deck, the screams of Weth and the laughing and jeering of the crew. They filled the space and only further highlighted how desperately I needed to get the fuck out of there— or I could be next.

I swung open every door that was below deck to check for any windows bigger than a porthole. There was only one room, the captain's quarters at the stern.

I headed straight for the window after closing the door behind me, but then thought, *This is his room. This could be the only way to learn who he truly is.*

I turned to the desk, intending on finding out anything, just one thing, about him that was true and ended up getting lost in documents, records, contracts with crew members—everything that a merchant would have, a privateer, a pirate.

I looked up from the desk in a daze. Helio was a pirate.

Goblin artifacts lined the walls: rich fabrics and jewels; heavy, ornate books; and expensive navigation tools; it was beyond appreciation or collection. I dug through the drawers of the desk, pulling out everything inside each one and throwing it to the ground, pocketing the occasional item out of spite—at least he'd told the truth about having hundreds of goblin bracelets—searching for the one item that almost every sea captain had. When I couldn't find it, I yelled in frustration and flipped the desk.

"Looking for this?" Helio asked from the doorway. He leaned against the frame, ankles crossed, captain's log in hand. He flipped it open to a random page and cleared his throat, "*'Captain's log of* The Bloody Maiden, *day two hundred and ten of year one hundred and sixty-two of King Methuselah the second's reign,'*" he read aloud. "*'Today I begin my journey to Shinchaku. The map piece has been seized by the Princess Bellona, of Carracalla, and my crew have confirmed her desire to discover its secrets. Thankfully, the Princess is not sailing with King Eevan, of Isidia, as I had first feared. This only makes my task easier. I shall meet her in Shinchaku as planned and, if all goes well, find passage on her ship and aid her in her journey. She is the last piece of the puzzle. I have lost too many to the beasts in the cavern and, despite many valiant efforts, to the pool. I believe only she can retrieve the bracelet from the bottom of the pool...'* Shall I continue?" he asked, eyebrow raised.

"It was all a lie," I seethed, my whole body shaking again.

He sighed and fully entered the room, closing the door behind him and locking it. "*Some* of it was a lie."

"No," I said, shaking my head. "*All* of it. Don't try to bullshit me now."

"Bell—"

"Don't you dare call me by my name when I don't even know yours!" I screamed. I didn't know if he'd lied about that, but something told me that he wouldn't have gone through everything we had using his true name.

"I planned to tell you," he said quietly, as if he meant it more for himself. "I did. I was going to tell you everything, but ..." His eyes flicked upward to the deck, as if something up there was to blame for his own failure.

"Don't try to redeem yourself now," I spat. "There's no coming back from this, *pirate.*"

He flinched. "Please, just give me the bracelet and I can let you leave. They won't care," he said, again gesturing to the deck above, as if his crew were the ones to fear, to blame. "As long as they have the bracelet, you can go," he pleaded.

"Fuck you." I punched through one of the windows behind me, the glass cut through the skin on my hand.

What looked like worry washed over Helio's face. His eyes shone with tears. "Bel—"

"Stop." I demanded. "Stop speaking." I pulled a bracelet from my pocket, its silver band glinting in the light shining through the windows. The pain from my hand was dizzying. I tried to concentrate a bit of magic there to at least stop the bleeding and numb it slightly, but I wanted him to see the injury. If he really cared about me, I wanted him to hurt. "Here's your fucking bracelet," I said, throwing it on the floor. "I hope it was worth it." I turned to jump through the window.

"Orrick!" He cried. "My name is Orrick Ubel."

I paused, taking one last look at him, at the charade he'd put on, the scholarly clothes he dressed in that probably belonged to a victim of his piracy, the ink stains that smattered his arms—now joined by specks of blood. His freckles and sun-kissed skin from long voyages. A tear finally slipped from the corner of my eye and, with it, a portion of my heart.

"Bellona ..."

I let him say it, if only to hear it on his lips one last time, and then I leapt from the window. The salt of my tears mixed with that of the sea as the only thing that my mind could do was repeat the betrayer's name.

Orrick Ubel. Orrick Ubel. Orrick Ubel.

CHAPTER
28

I'd been traveling below water for days, my journey sped up with some help from friends that dwelled beneath the waves. I didn't speak to them, didn't ask, they simply saw me and offered a fin, a tentacle, a tail, and soon enough I came upon a hull I'd recognize anywhere. She was pristine, absolutely barnacle free, and shining beneath the waves. The sight of her brought me to tears. I swam to her as she cut her way through the waves and, with much difficulty, climbed the Jacob's ladder, collapsing onto the deck as I reached the top.

"Captain!" Cerys exclaimed as she almost stood on me. "We were on our way to find you—just crossed the Osirian border a few days ago."

I hauled myself to my feet. Everyone on the ship had stopped what they were doing and stared at me. I was grateful to see them all, more grateful than they could ever understand. Then, reflexively, I reached back, as if I were waiting to help someone else climb aboard, and I was reminded of everything that had happened, everything that had led to this moment and rage and sadness filled me.

"Captain, are you alright?" Cerys asked.

"Do I look alright?!" I snapped. Everyone straightened, including Cerys. "Get back to work, you lot of bilge rats!" I yelled, throwing down my wet pack and leaving it for someone else to pick up and deal with. "Someone get me a drink. A proper fucking drink!" I ordered and stalked to my cabin. It was blissfully empty, though it wouldn't be soon, and I desperately needed a drink to get through the conversations I was about to be forced into. I pulled out a trunk from under my bed with all of my nicer wines and spirits from around the world, ones I saved for special occasions or guests. I selected a bottle at random, pulled the cork out with my teeth, and downed half the bottle in one long chug before my brother burst through the door.

His eyes fell on the bottle, then he took in the state of me and closed the door behind him, latching the lock into place as he did.

"You were right," I croaked out, the spirit having burned the surface of my throat. "He couldn't be trusted."

"Bell ..." Peverell said, stepping closer to me with his arms out.

"He didn't even tell me his true name," I rambled. "It was all bullshit!" I threw the half-empty bottle at the floor. It shattered, coating me and Peverell in the clear liquid and leaving shards of jagged glass all over the floor. "He was a fucking pirate." My head was swaying, the room spinning. Peverell seemed to stay in one place, but everything else moved around him and wouldn't stop. "He fucking lied to me," I whispered.

"I take it you didn't make it to Osiria," Peverell said, clearly unsure of how to approach the situation.

"Oh no, we made it to Osiria. I almost died. Wolvane tore people apart, guardians and fucking trolls attacked us. I almost drowned."

"What?!"

"He told me he loved me." I picked up another bottle and screamed wordlessly as I threw it against the wall.

Peverell shielded his eyes as the glass and contents spilled out across the room.

"He ... he fucking lied." I knew I was repeating myself, could hear it in my mind, but my mouth couldn't say anything else. *He lied, he fucking lied*, were the only words my lips could form. My eyes started to droop. I was so tired, mentally and physically, I could fall asleep where I stood.

Then something popped into my mind. "I fucking got him though," I said, stepping toward Peverell and jabbing a finger into his chest. He placed a hand on either of my shoulders to steady me. "I fucking lied to him!" I shoved a hand into my swimming clothes and pulled out Peverell's little notebook. The pages were fat and wet, the ink smudged to the point of illegible. "Oh, Pev," I said sadly, "I ruined it."

"What did you lie to him about Bellona?" Peverell asked, ignoring his notebook.

"I have the bracelet," I whispered. "He thought I gave it back, but it was a bullshit one." I laughed to myself, almost going limp in my brother's arms, and he grunted as he pulled me back to my feet.

"You have the bracelet?" he asked.

"It's in the book!" I said, offended that he hadn't figured it out yet.

"Oh, Bell." He pulled me into a tight hug and, for some reason, that was my undoing.

I couldn't stand any longer. I couldn't breathe—gasping at the air like a fish out of water, but none would enter my lungs. The tears slid down my face, but I couldn't get the air I needed to cry. Couldn't get my lungs to work. They burned, restricting the air until my head grew foggy. Then, all at once, they pulled in too much air and I choked on it—coughed—and repeated that same process for the Mother and Father knew how many times. Peverell held my face in his hands, begging me to breathe, telling me everything was going to be alright. He was lying, too. Nothing was going to be alright.

CHAPTER
29

The voyage back to Isidia was a drunken blur. I left my cabin only two or three times to retrieve more drink, leaving the ship entirely under Jarrel's command. He tried his best to make it feel as if I were still making decisions, as if I still had purpose and reason to be there, but his attempts did little to improve my mood.

I'd slid back into old habits so quickly and with such force that you'd never have believed I'd quit them at all. The conditions set forth by Islina were always circulating in my thoughts. I wanted to see my niece, to be part of her life—more than anything—but I found myself always making concessions and excuses. *One more drink won't hurt. Islina will never know. I've been through enough.*

Then, I would spiral even further. *What example am I setting? Would she want to know me at all? Would I let someone like me near her?* And then a whole bottle would be consumed and I'd be throwing up down the stern of *The Siren*.

I didn't leave the ship once we made berth. I stayed in my stale room and drank myself even further into a stupor. People came in to speak with me, but I could barely make them out through the blur of drunkenness. I don't know what I said to any of them, or if my words were coherent at all—I doubted it.

Then, one day, the drinks stopped coming. No one answered my calls, my demands, my pleas. I got up from my pile of bedding on the floor and stalked to the door, but after I reached it, the handle would turn but the door would not open. I slammed my fist against the wood until it was swollen and tender. I screamed at the door until my throat was hoarse, and then I sobbed against it.

I was sweating, nauseous, head pounding, and curled back on top of my bedding pile when finally someone came through the door. I didn't have the energy left to open my eyes and see who it was, nor did I have the capacity to care. They joined me on the bedding and lifted my head onto their lap, brushing my sweat-soaked hair from my face with delicate fingers.

"Islina?" I croaked

"Peverell says you did well … until the end," she whispered.

"I tried," I said, my eyes welling.

"I know," she soothed, gently stroking my cheek. "Peverell told us everything—well, what he knew."

"Why are you here?" I asked, not knowing what else to say.

"I forced you to do this to yourself, so I should view the consequences."

"No," I said firmly. "*I* did this to myself. I always do this to myself."

"Do you?" she questioned, "or are you forced into it by the positions others put you in? Is it a reputation you've made for yourself or that others have placed on you?"

I didn't know what to say. My mind screamed that it was my fault, I was the problem. But some small part of me could see sense in her words and tried desperately to convince the rest that it was wrong about itself. The youngest of a royal line is always considered disposable, and though my family never made me feel it, I knew it to be true.

There was so much pressure placed on Darius and Peverell; Eevan and I never had that. We were free to do as we wished, and we had, for centuries. Until Eevan had managed to convince Islina he was a good match for her. Then I was completely alone. Unsupervised. What little regard there was for my safety and behavior previously only further dissipated, and maybe, just maybe, that wouldn't have happened if someone had just shown interest, concern, literally any kind of attention toward me. But I was not selfish enough to lay blame completely onto my family. They didn't force me to drink and smoke, to make stupid decisions and disregard my own safety, but they also hadn't stepped in—and probably never would have.

I met Islina's eyes and wanted to shrink away from the glint of hope that shone in them. I'd always felt as if she hated me, but also that she could somehow read my mind, as if my brother and I were so similar that in deciphering his mind she had also learned the secrets of mine.

The door banged against the wall behind us and Eevan crashed through it.

"Where is the baby?" Islina demanded.

"With my parents, she's fine," he insisted, coming to kneel beside me and Islina. "Bell, I'm sorry. I shouldn't have encouraged you to go. You should have stayed here until you were sober."

"That has nothing to do with this," I said, weakly gesturing toward myself. Eevan's presence calmed me more than I thought anything could, and I was able to tell him everything. Everything about the traps in the temple and the city, breaking into the tower and Helio … Orrick, I told him everything about Orrick. Islina squeezed my hand as I recounted the moment I learned who he really was, what he really was, and that the whole journey had happened because of his manipulation and design. Eevan's expression was sympathetic for only a moment before he exploded into a rage. He shot to his feet and began pacing the length of my cabin, running his fingers up and down the bridge of his nose.

"I warned Methuselah about this," he said. "I told him there'd be an uprising of pirates after the ridiculous way he ran his navy. Did he listen?!"

"That's assuming the Osirians even read the letters, Eevan," Islina said. "You have to remember you're the King of Isidia now—they'll only hear so much from us."

"But on a matter such as this?!"

"Especially on matters such as this," Islina said firmly. "Why do you think I needed so much assistance from your family? The Osirians wanted nothing to do with me, would not respond to any of my letters, would not agree to meet. I thought it would change once Methuselah took the throne from his mother but, if anything, the contact has only gotten worse—especially since the birth of the heir."

"The human pirates are nuisance enough, but Osirian pirates." He shook his head. "They'll rule the seas before long."

"One crew does not mean there are more," I rasped.

"Of course it does, Bellona," Eevan said gently, ceasing his pacing and squatting down beside me. "Pirates are like rats," he said sternly, "where there is one in the open, there are thousands hidden." He took my hand and gave it a light squeeze before he closed his eyes as he sucked in a breath, as though he knew I would not like what he was to say next. "Do not let this ... entanglement cloud your judgment. He is a pirate. He betrayed you, and he would no doubt do it again."

They were the words I needed to hear, but it didn't stop them from hurting. I clenched my jaw in an effort to hold in my tears as Eevan continued. "I will send one more letter to Osiria. If I hear nothing in return and nothing is done, I will personally take on the task of ridding the seas of pirates. Even if it leads to a war."

"Eevan!" Islina snapped. "I don't want another war with the Osirians."

"Then maybe their King should do something about his people," Eevan snapped back. "I am not going to sit on this throne and allow my people, our people, my *family*, to be terrorized by pirates or Osirians. I will end it. This feud with them ends with our rule, Islina. I will *not* have this drag on and leave it for our daughter to deal with." Islina opened her mouth to argue and closed it as Eevan raised a hand. "She is the eldest. She will rule. I will not argue this."

I'd never heard Eevan be so stern with Islina and suddenly felt extremely awkward. They stared at each other for a long while, having some kind of silent argument.

"I don't need you to fight my battles for me, Eevan." I said, unable to handle the silence any longer.

Eevan thought on this for a moment before saying, "Then I will leave Orrick for you. But if you can't do it, I will."

I nodded, knowing that I couldn't argue with him. If there was one thing Eevan would not let stand, it was attacks against his family. It didn't matter who it was, Eevan would get his revenge.

"Well, I've had enough of all this," Islina finally said, letting my head drop from her lap gently as she slowly rose to her feet, her usual cool demeanor settling back into place. "Bellona," her tone was no longer soft as she addressed me, "you will stay with us at the palace until *I* deem you recovered. There will be *no* arguing, *no* sneaking out, and *no* running away. Otherwise, you will face the same consequences as our previous arrangement." She looked down at me. "Agreed?"

I glanced at Eevan, the rage still visible behind his eyes, but hopefulness was at the forefront. "Agreed."

I sighed, but smiled as Islina did quickly before she turned away and said as she left the room, "It stinks in here, Bellona, You really should have it cleaned."

Eevan and I exhaled in exasperation. It was going to be a long and slow recovery, especially while dealing with Islina, but Eevan was here for the journey with me.

"Did Peverell give you the bracelet?" I asked, slowly rising to a sitting position.

"He did." Eevan paused for a moment, his hand dipping into his pocket. "We decided it was best kept in your possession," he said, pulling the silver bangle from his jacket and flicking it into my lap. I stared at it. "We're too connected to larger kingdoms, and I feel this could give us an unfair advantage in war."

"Isn't that what you want in war?"

Eevan shook his head. "There's tactical and there's unfair. I'm not one to be unfair, but we both know that Darius could be. It's best that the bracelet's existence and abilities are kept between the three of us."

"Agreed," I said, my mind wandering back to what Helio—*Orrick*, had said about the bracelet and the fairies trying to escape the forest. "But should we ever need it, I will not hesitate."

Eevan nodded.

"How is our brother?" I asked.

"I don't know what you guys did to Pev, but I've never seen him so lively," Eevan said as he hoisted me to my feet. My stomach lurched, but I held in the vomit that tried to escape as I wrapped an arm around his shoulder and leaned my weight onto him. "He hasn't stopped talking the whole time he's been back, and I don't think I've seen him in the library once."

"I wouldn't let him near any libraries if I were you. He's a book thief."

Eevan laughed. "Oh, I know. There are always volumes missing after he visits." He stopped laughing and leaned closer to me as we stepped out of my darkened cabin onto the sun-lit deck, my crew nowhere to be seen, but he whispered anyway, "Are he and Jarrel … ?"

I groaned, already longing for a drink.

ACKNOWLEDGEMENTS

Again, the first people that deserve any kind of acknowledgements are my partner and son. They deal with so much crap while I'm planning, writing and editing, and with such patience. I'm pretty sure they've both wanted to kill me multiple times during the production of this book, and I thank them for not.

Big thank you to Hayley for your sea monster illustration! He's absolutely perfect.

Another big thank you to Danikka Taylor for being the best editor ever! My books would be a complete mess without your editing magic.

Thank you to my amazingly supportive readers and friends, without you guys I would have given up.

Special thank you to Zamira! For being especially amazing from day one and always posting and talking about my book. I appreciate you so much.

ABOUT THE AUTHOR

E. A. Olivieri never thought she'd be an author, but, after writing out of boredom while on maternity leave, she discovered a passion for it.

She loves all things dark and fantastical, and channels that through her writing.

When E. A. isn't creating new worlds, she's working on an art project or playing video games with her son and partner in their West Australian home.

Scan this code for more information on where to purchase books and how to follow the author.

WANT MORE?
READ EVALINA'S STORY IN...

ASHWOOD AND BRIMSTONE

Coming Soon...

ALABASTER

AND

OBSIDIAN

A CARYNTHIA NOVEL

www.ingramcontent.com/pod-product-compliance
Lightning Source LLC
Chambersburg PA
CBHW030532130626
46552CB00006B/2224